ROGER ZELAZNY

FOUR FOR TOMORROW

This is a work of fiction. All the characters and events portrayed in this book are fictional, and any resemblance to real people or incidents is purely coincidental.

Copyright © 1967 by Roger Zelazny
The Furies, copyright ©, 1965, by Ziff-Davis Publishing Co.
The Graveyard Heart, copyright ©, 1964, by Ziff-Davis Publishing Co.
The Doors of His Face, the Lamps of His Mouth, copyright ©, 1965, by Mercury Press, Inc.
A Rose for Ecclesiastes, copyright ©, 1963, by Mercury Press, Inc.

All rights reserved, including the right to reproduce this book or portions thereof in any form.

A Baen Book

Baen Publishing Enterprises
P.O. Box 1403
Riverdale, N.Y. 10471

ISBN: 0-671-72051-1

Cover art by Debbie Hughes

First Baen printing, April 1991

Distributed by
SIMON & SCHUSTER
1230 Avenue of the Americas
New York, N.Y. 10020

Printed in the United States of America

AUTHOR'S DEDICATION:

To My Mother

Contents

Introduction	1
The Furies	9
The Graveyard Heart	55
The Doors of His Face, The Lamps of His Mouth	125
A Rose for Ecclesiastes	167

INTRODUCTION

by Theodore Sturgeon

There has been nothing like Zelazny in the science fiction field since—

Thus began the first draft of this introduction and there it stayed for about forty-eight hours while I maundered and chuntered on ways to finish that sentence with justice and precision. The only possible way to do it is to knock off the last word. And even then it misses the truth, for the term "science fiction" gives the comment a kind of club membership which trims verity. So much which is published as science fiction is nothing of the kind. And more and more, science fiction is produced and not called science fiction (and paid for heartily—i.e. *On the Beach, Dr. Strangelove, Seven Days in May, 1984*, etc., etc., et al.—which makes the pro science fiction writers candidates for persecution mania). Suffice it for now to say that you'll be hard put to it to find a writer like Zelazny anywhere.

Genuine prose-poets we have seen, but quite often they fail when the measures of pace and structure are applied. And we have certainly had truly great storytellers, whose narrative architecture is solidly based, soundly built, and well-braced clear to tower-tip; but more often than not, this is done completely with a homogenized, nuts-and-bolts kind of prose. And there has been a regrettably small handful of what I call "people experts"—those especially gifted to create memorable characters, something more than real ones well-photographed . . . *living* ones who change, as all living things change, not only during the reading, but in the memory as the reader himself lives and changes and becomes capable of bringing more of himself to that which the writer has brought him. But there again, "people experts" have a tendency to turn their rare gift into a preoccupation (and create small ardent cliques who tend to the same thing) and skimp on matters of structure and content. An apt analogy would be a play superbly cast and skilfully mounted, for which somebody had forgotten to supply a script.

And if you think I am about to say that Zelazny delivers all these treasures and avoids all these oversights, that he has full measures of substance and structure, means and ends, texture, cadence and pace, you are absolutely right.

Three factors in Zelazny's work call for isolation and examination; and the very cold-bloodedness of such a declamation demands amendment. Let me revise it to two and a pointing finger, a vague and inarticulate wave toward something Out (or Up, or In) There which can be analyzed about as effectively as the internal effect of watching the color-shift on the skin of a bubble or that silent explosion somewhere inside the midriff which is one of the recognitions of love.

First, Zelazny's stories are fabulous. I use this

word in a special and absolutely accurate sense. Aesop did not, and did not intend to, convey a factual account of an improbably vegetarian fox equipped with speech and with human value judgments concerning a bunch of unreachable grapes. He was saying something else and something larger than what he said. And it has come to me over the years that the greatness of literature and the importance of literary entities (Captain Ahab, Billy Budd, Hamlet, Job, Uriah Heep) really lies in this fabulous quality. One may ponderously call them Jungian archetypes, but one recognizes them, and/or their situational predicaments, in one's own daily contacts with this landlord, that employer, and one's dearly beloved. A fable says more than it says, is bigger than its own parameters. Zelazny always says more than he says; all of his yarns have applications, illuminate truths, donate to the reader tools (and sometimes weapons) with which he was not equipped before, and for which he can find daily uses, quite outside the limits of his story.

Second, there is, as one reads more and more of this extraordinary writer's work, a growing sense of excitement, a gradual recognition of something which (in me, anyway) engenders an increasing awe. It comes, strangely enough, not from any of his many excellences, but from his flaws. For he has flaws—plenty of them. One feels at times that a few (a very few, I hasten to add) of his more vivid turns of phrase would benefit by an application of Dulcote (an artists' material, a transparent spray which uniformly pulls down brightness and gloss where applied). Not because they aren't beautiful—because most of them are, God knows—but because even so deft a wordsmith as Zelazny can forget from time to time that such a creation can keep a reader from his speedy progress from here to there, and that his furniture should be placed out of the traffic pattern. If I bang my shin on a coffee table it becomes a little beside the point that it is the most exquisitely crafted artifact this side of the Sun King. Especially since it was the author himself who put me in a dead run. And there is the matter of exotic references—the injection of one of those absolutely precise and therefore untranslatable German philosophic terms, or a citation from classical mythology. This is a difficult thing to criticize without being misunderstood. A really good writer has the right, if not the duty, of arrogance, and should feel free to say anythng he damn pleases in any way he likes. On the other hand, writing, like elections, copulation, sonatas, or a punch in the mouth, is *communication,* an absolute necessity to the very existence of human beings in every area, concrete or abstract, which may be defined as that performed by human beings which evokes response *in kind* from other human beings. Communication is a double-ended, transmitter-receiver phenomenon or it doesn't exist. And if it evokes a response not in kind ("what the hell does *that* mean?" instead of "well of course!") it exists but it is crippled. There is a fine line, and hazy, between following the use of an exotic intrusion with a definition, which can be damned insulting to a reader who does understand it, and throwing him something knobby and hard to hold without warning or subsequent explanation. Yes, a reader *should* do part of the work; the more he does the more he participates, and the more he is led to participate the better the story (and writer). On the other hand, he shouldn't be stopped, thrown out of the current in which the author has placed him, by such menaces to navigation, however apt. It comes down to an awareness of who's listening—to whom the communication is addressed—and what he deserves. He deserves a great deal, because he's at the other end of something which could not exist without him. Those of him (for he is many) who need pampering do *not* deserve it. Those who can take anything a really good author can throw at him are an author's joy—but always a small part of that multifaceted and very human entity, The Reader. There is always, for a resourceful writer, a way to maximize communication by means acceptable to a writer's arrogance; all he has to do is to think of it. In a writer less resourceful than Zelazny we readily forgive his inability to think of it, but this writer doesn't have that excuse. Which brings this comment down to its point: Roger Zelazny is a writer of such merit that one judges him by higher standards than those one uses on others—a cross he will bear for all his writing life. Happily, the shoulders that bear it are demonstrably well-muscled.

The larger point, derived from this consideration of flaws, has to do with the kind of flaws they are. For in none of the things I have mentioned, nor in the ones I could, is a single one stemming from inability. Every single one is the product of growth, expansion, trial, passage, flux. There is nothing so frightening to be said about a writer (although some writers are not frightened by it) as the laudatory comment "finish." A perfectly faceted diamond is beautiful to behold, and is by its very existence proof of high skill and hard work; but it has nowhere to go, intrinsically, from there. A great tree reaches its ultimate "finish" when it is killed; and it may then become toothpicks or temples, but as a tree it is dead and gone. Only that which is in constant, day-by-day, cell-by-cell change is alive. And it is in this area that I have detected and increasingly feel a sense of awe in Zelazny's work, for he is young and already a giant; he has the habit of hard work and of learning, and shows no slightest sign of slowing down or of being diverted. I do not know him personally, but if I did, if I ever do, I would want more than anything else to convey to him the fact that he can and has evoked this awe—that the curve he has drawn with his early work can be extended into true greatness, and that if he follows his star as a writer all other things will come to him. If ever anything seems more important to him—he must know that it isn't. If ever anything diverts him from writing, he must know to the marrow that whatever it is or appears to be, it is a lesser thing than his gift. He gives no evidence to date that he has stopped growing or that he ever will.

Do you know how rare this is?

The four stories in this book, listed here by my own intensely personal (and therefore, to you, perhaps fallible) system of ascending excellence, are all of that wondrous species which makes me envy anyone who has not read them and is about to.

The Doors of His Face, the Lamps of His Mouth is all size and speed, which would be a good story if told purely in a write-what-happens, this-is-the-plot style, and which would also be a good story if it confined itself to what went on in the heads and in the hearts of its people, and which is a good story on both counts.

The Furies is a *tour de force*, the easy accomplishment of what most writers would consider impossible, and a few very good ones insuperably difficult. Seemingly with the back of his hand, he has created *milieu*, characters and a narrative goal as far out as anyone need go; he makes you believe it all the way, and walks off breathing easily leaving you gasping with a fable in your hands.

The Graveyard Heart is in that wonderful category

which is, probably, science fiction's greatest gift to literature and to human beings: the "feedback" story, the "if this goes on" story; an extension of some facet of the current scene which carries you out and away to times and places you've never imagined because you can't; and when it's finished, you turn about and look at the thing he extended for you, in its here-and-now reality, sharing this very day and planet with you; and you know he's told you something, given you something you didn't have before, and that you will never look at this aspect of your world with quite the same eyes again.

A Rose for Ecclesiastes is one of the most important stories I have read—perhaps I should say it is one of the most memorable experiences I have ever had. It happens (well, I *told* you this was an intensely personal assignment of rank!) that this particular fable, with all its truly astonishing twists and turns, up to and most painfully including its wrenching denouement, is an agonizing analogy of my own experience; and this astronomically unlikely happenstance may well make it what it is to me and may not reach you quite as poignantly. If it does it will chop you up into dog meat. But as objective as I can be, which isn't very, I still feel safe in stating that it is one of the most beautifully written, skillfully composed and passionately expressed works of art to appear anywhere, ever.

Briefly, let me commend to your attention two novels by Roger Zelazny, *This Immortal* and *The Dream Master,** and sum up everything I have said here, and a good many things I have not said; sum up all the thoughts and feelings I hold concerning the works of Roger Zelazny, past and to come; sum

*Both Baen Books.

up what has struck me at each of the peaks of all of his narratives, and without fail, so far, at that regretful moment when I have turned down the last page of any and all of them; sum up all this in one word, which is:

Grateful.

Theodore Sturgeon
Sherman Oaks, California.

The Furies

As an afterthought, Nature sometimes tosses a bone to those it maims and casts aside. Often, it is in the form of a skill, usually useless, or the curse of intelligence.

When Sandor Sandor was four years old he could name all the 149 inhabited worlds in the galaxy. When he was five he could name the principal land masses of each planet and chalk them in, roughly, on blank globes. By the time he was seven years old he knew all the provinces, states, countries and major cities of all the main land masses on all 149 inhabited worlds in the galaxy. He read Landography, History, Landology and popular travel guides during most of his waking time; and he studied maps and travel tapes. There was a camera behind his eyes, or so it seemed, because by the time he was ten years old there was no city in the galaxy that anyone could name about which Sandor Sandor did not know *something*.

And he continued.

Places fascinated him. He built a library of street guides, road maps. He studied architectural styles and principal industries, and racial types, native lifeforms, local flora, landmarks, hotels, restaurants, airports and seaports and spaceports, styles of clothing and personal ornamentation, climatic conditions, local arts and crafts, dietary habits, sports, religions, social institutions, customs.

When he took his doctorate in Landography at the age of fourteen, his oral examinations were conducted via closed circuit television. This is because he was afraid to leave his home—having done so only three times before in his life and having met with fresh trauma on each occasion. And *this* is because on all 149 inhabited worlds in the galaxy there was no remedy for a certain degenerative muscular disease. This disease made it impossible for Sandor to manipulate even the finest prosthetic devices for more than a few minutes without suffering fatigue and great pain; and to go outside he required three such devices—two legs and a right arm—to substitute for those which he had missed out on receiving somewhere along the line before birth.

Rather than suffer this pain, or the pain of meeting persons other than his Aunt Faye or his nurse, Miss Barbara, he took his oral examinations via closed circuit television.

The University of Brill, Dombeck, was located on the other side of that small planet from Sandor's home, else the professors would have come to see *him*, because they respected him considerably. His 855-page dissertation, "Some Notes Toward a Gravitational Matrix Theory Governing the Formation of Similar Land Masses on Dissimilar Planetary Bodies," had drawn attention from Interstel University on Earth itself. Sandor Sandor, of course, would never see the Earth. His muscles could only sustain the gravitation of smaller planets, such as Dombeck.

And it happened that the Interstel Government, which monitors everything, had listened in on Sandor's oral examinations and his defense of his dissertation.

Associate Professor Baines was one of Sandor's very few friends. They had even met several times in person, in Sandor's library, because Baines often said he'd wanted to borrow certain books and then came and spent the afternoon. When the examinations were concluded, Associate Professor Baines stayed on the circuit for several minutes, talking with Sandor. It was during this time that Baines made casual reference to an almost useless (academically, that is) talent of Sandor's.

At the mention of it, the government man's ears had pricked forward (he was a Rigellian). He was anxious for a promotion and he recalled an obscure memo. . . .

Associate Professor Baines had mentioned the fact that Sandor Sandor had once studied a series of thirty random photos from all over the civilized galaxy, and that the significant data from these same photos had also been fed into the Department's L-L computer. Sandor had named the correct planet in each case, the land mass in twenty-nine, the county or territory in twenty-six, and he had correctly set the location itself within fifty square miles in twenty-three instances. The L-L comp had named the correct planet for twenty-seven.

It was not a labor of love for the computer.

So it became apparent that Sandor Sandor knew just about every damn street in the galaxy.

Ten years later he knew them all.

But three years later the Rigellian quit his job, disgusted, and went to work in private industry, where the pay was better and promotions more frequent. *His* memo, and the tape, had been filed, however. . . .

Benedick Benedict was born and grew up on the watery world of Kjum, and his was an infallible power for making enemies of everyone he met.

The reason why is that while some men's highest pleasure is drink, and others are given to gluttony, and still others are slothful, or lechery is their chief delight, or *Phrinn*-doing, Benedick's was gossip—he was a loudmouth.

Gossip was his meat and his drink, his sex and his religion. Shaking hands with him was a mistake, often a catastrophic one. For, as he clung to your hand, pumping it and smiling, his eyes would suddenly grow moist and the tears would dribble down his fat cheeks.

He wasn't sad when this happened. Far from it. It was a somatic conversion from his paranorm reaction.

He was seeing your past life.

He was selective, too; he only saw what he looked for. And he looked for scandal and hate, and what is often worse, love; he looked for lawbreaking and unrest, for memories of discomfort, pain, futility, weakness. He saw everything a man wanted to forget, and he talked about it.

If you are lucky he won't tell you of your own. If you have ever met someone else whom he has also met in this manner, and if this fact shows, he will begin talking of *that* person. He will tell you of that man's or woman's life because he appreciates this form of social reaction even more than your outrage at yourself. And his eyes and voice and hand will hold you, like the clutch of the Ancient Mariner, in a sort of half dream-state; and you will hear him out and you will be shocked beneath your paralysis.

Then he will go away and tell others about you.

Such a man was Benedick Benedict. He was probably unaware how much he was hated, because this reaction never came until later, after he had said "Good day," departed, and been gone for several hours. He left his hearers with a just-raped feeling— and later fear, shame, or disgust forced them to suppress the occurrence and to try to forget him. Or else they hated him quietly, because he was dangerous. That is to say, he had powerful friends.

He was an extremely social animal: he loved attention; he wanted to be admired; he craved audiences.

He could always find an audience too, somewhere. He knew so many secrets that he was tolerated in important places in return for the hearing. And he was wealthy too, but more of that in a moment.

As time went on, it became harder and harder for him to meet new people. His reputation spread in geometric proportion to his talking, and even those who would hear him preferred to sit on the far side of the room, drink enough alcohol to partly deaden memories of themselves, and to be seated near a door.

The reason for his wealth is because his power extended to inanimate objects as well. Minerals were rare on Kjum, the watery world. If anyone brought him a sample he could hold it and weep and tell them where to dig to hit the main lode.

From one fish caught in the vast seas of Kjum, he could chart the course of a school of fish.

Weeping, he could touch a native rad-pearl necklace and divine the location of the native's rad-pearl bed.

Local insurance associations and loan companies kept Benedict Files—the pen a man had used to sign his contract, his snubbed-out cigarette butt, a plastex hanky with which he had mopped his brow, an object left in security, the remains of a biopsy or blood test—so that Benedick could use his power against those who renege on these companies and flee, on those who break their laws.

He did not revel in his power either. He simply enjoyed it. For he was one of the nineteen known paranorms in the 149 inhabited worlds in the galaxy, and he knew no other way.

Also, he occasionally assisted civil authorities, if he thought their cause a just one. If he did not, he suddenly lost his power until the need for it vanished. This didn't happen too often though, for an humanitarian was Benedick Benedict, and well-paid, because he was laboratory-tested and clinically-proven. He could psychometrize. He could pick up thought-patterns originating outside his own skull. . . .

Lynx Links looked like a beach ball with a beard, a fat patriarch with an eye patch, a man who loved good food and drink, simple clothing, and the company of simple people; he was a man who smiled often and whose voice was soft and melodic.

In his earlier years he had chalked up the most impressive kill-record of any agent ever employed by Interstel Central Intelligence. Forty-eight men and seventeen malicious alien life-forms had the Lynx dispatched during his fifty-year tenure as a field agent. He was one of the three men in the galaxy to have lived through half a century's employment with ICI. He lived comfortably on his government pension despite three wives and a horde of grandchildren; he was recalled occasionally as a consultant; and he did some part-time missionary work on the side. He believed that all life was one and that all men were brothers, and that love rather than hate or fear should rule the affairs of men. He had even killed with love, he often remarked at Tranquility Session, respecting and revering the person and the spirit of the man who had been marked for death.

This is the story of how he came to be summoned

back from Hosanna, the World of the Great and Glorious Flame of the Divine Life, and was joined with Sandor Sandor and Benedick Benedict in the hunt for Victor Corgo, the man without a heart.

Victor Corgo was captain of the *Wallaby*. Victor Corgo was Head Astrogator, First Mate, and Chief Engineer of the *Wallaby*. Victor Corgo *was* the *Wallaby*.

One time the *Wallaby* was a proud Guardship, an ebony toadstool studded with the jewel-like warts of fast-phrase projectors. One time the *Wallaby* skipped proud about the frontier worlds of Interstel, meting out the unique justice of the Uniform Galactic Code—in those places where there was no other law. One time the proud *Wallaby*, under the command of Captain Victor Corgo of the Guard, had ranged deep space and become a legend under legendary skies.

A terror to brigands and ugly aliens, a threat to Codebreakers, and a thorn in the sides of evildoers everywhere, Corgo and his shimmering fungus (which could burn an entire continent under water level within a single day) were the pride of the Guard, the best of the best, the cream that had been skimmed from all the rest.

Unfortunately, Corgo sold out.

He became a heel.

. . . A traitor.

A hero gone bad . . .

After forty-five years with the Guard, his pension but half a decade away, he lost his entire crew in an ill-timed raid upon a pirate stronghold on the planet Kilsh, which might have become the 150th inhabited world of Interstel.

Crawling, barely alive, he had made his way half across the great snowfield of Brild, on the main land mass of Kilsh. At the fortuitous moment, Death making its traditional noises of approach, he was snatched from out its traffic lane, so to speak, by the Drillen, a nomadic tribe of ugly and intelligent quadrupeds, who took him to their camp and healed his wounds, fed him, and gave him warmth. Later, with the cooperation of the Drillen, he recovered the *Wallaby* and all its arms and armaments, from where it had burnt its way to a hundred feet beneath the ice.

Crewless, he trained the Drillen.

With the Drillen and the *Wallaby* he attacked the pirates.

He won.

But he did not stop with that.

No.

When he learned that the Drillen had been marked for death under the Uniform Code, he sold out his own species. The Drillen had refused relocation to a decent Reservation World. They had elected to continue occupancy of what was to become the 150th inhabited world in the galaxy (that is to say, in Interstel).

Therefore, the destruct-order had been given.

Captain Corgo protested, was declared out of order.

Captain Corgo threatened, was threatened in return.

Captain Corgo fought, was beaten, died, was resurrected, escaped restraint, became an outlaw.

He took the *Wallaby* with him. The *Happy Wallaby*, it had been called in the proud days. Now, it was just the *Wallaby*.

As the tractor beams had seized it, as the vibrations penetrated its ebony hull and tore at his flesh, Corgo had called his six Drillen to him, stroked the fur of Mala, his favorite, opened his mouth to speak, and died just as the words and the tears began.

"I am sorry . . ." he had said.

They gave him a new heart, though. His old one had fibrillated itself to pieces and could not be repaired. They put the old one in a jar and gave him a shiny, antiseptic egg of throbbing metal, which expanded and contracted at varying intervals, dependent upon what the seed-sized computers they had planted within him told of his breathing and his blood sugar and the output of his various glands. The seeds and the egg contained his life.

When they were assured that this was true and that it would continue, they advised him of the proceedings of courts-martial.

He did not wait, however, for due process. Breaking his parole as an officer, he escaped the Guard Post, taking with him Mala, the only remaining Drillen in the galaxy. Her five fellows had not survived scientific inquiry as to the nature of their internal structures. The rest of the race, of course, had refused relocation.

Then did the man without a heart make war upon mankind.

Raping a planet involves considerable expense. Enormous blasters and slicers and sluicers and refiners are required to reduce a world back almost to a state of primal chaos, and then to extract from it its essential (i.e., commercially viable) ingredients. The history books may tell you of strip-mining on the mother planet, back in ancient times. Well, the crude processes employed then were similar in emphasis and results, but the operations were considerably smaller in scale.

Visualize a hundred miles of Grand Canyon appearing overnight; visualize the reversal of thousands of Landological millenia in the twinkling of an eye; consider all the Ice Ages of the Earth, and compress them into a single season. This will give you a rough idea as to time and effect.

Now picture the imported labor—the men who drill and blast and slice and sluice for the great mining combines: Not uneducated, these men; willing to take a big risk, certainly though, these men—

maybe only for one year, because of the high pay; or maybe they're careerists, because of the high pay—these men, who hit three worlds in a year's time, who descend upon these worlds in ships full of city, in space-trailer mining camps, out of the sky; coming, these men, from all over the inhabited galaxy, bringing with them the power of the tool and the opposed thumb, bearing upon their brows the mark of the Solar Phoenix and in their eyes the cold of the spaces they have crossed over, they know what to do to make the domes of atoms rise before them and to call down the tornado-probosci of suck-vortices from the freighters on the other side of the sky; and they do it thoroughly and efficiently, and not without style, tradition, folksongs, and laughter—for they are the sweat-crews, working against time (which is money), to gain tonnage (which is money), and to beat their competitors to market (which is important, inasmuch as one worldsworth influences future sales for many months); these men, who bear in one hand the flame and in the other the whirlwind, who come down with their families and all their possessions, erect temporary metropoli, work their magic act, and go—after the vanishing trick has been completed.

Now that you've an idea as to what happens and who is present at the scene, here's the rub:

Raping a planet involves considerable expense.

The profits are more than commensurate, do not misunderstand. It is just that they could be even greater. . . .

How?

Well— For one thing, the heavy machinery involved is quite replaceable, in the main. That is, the machinery which is housed within the migrant metropoli.

Moving it is expensive. Not moving it isn't. For it is actually cheaper, in terms of material and labor, to manufacture new units than it is to fast-phase the old ones more than an average of 2.6 times.

Mining combines do not produce them (and wouldn't really want to); the mining manufacturing combines like to make new units as much as the mining combines like to lose old ones.

And of course it is rented machinery, or machinery on which payments are still being made, to the financing associations, because carrying payments makes it easier to face down the Interstel Revenue Service every fiscal year.

Abandoning the units would be criminal, violating either the lessor-lessee agreement or the Interstel Commercial Code.

But accidents do happen . . .

Often, too frequently to make for comfortable statistics . . .

Way out there on the raw frontier.

Then do the big insurance associations investigate, and they finally sigh and reimburse the lien-holders.

. . . And the freighters make it to market ahead of schedule, because there is less to dismantle and march-order and ship.

Time is saved, commitments are met in advance, a better price is generally obtained, and a head start on the next worldsworth is supplied in this manner.

All of which is nice.

Except for the insurance associations.

But what can happen to a transitory New York full of heavy equipment?

Well, some call it sabotage.

. . . Some call it mass-murder.

. . . Unsanctioned war.

. . . .Corgo's lightning.

But it is written that it is better to burn one city than to curse the darkness.

Corgo did not curse the darkness.

. . . Many times.

* * *

The day they came together on Dombeck, Benedick held forth his hand, smiled, said: "Mister Sandor . . ."

As his hand was shaken, his smile reversed itself. Then it went away from his face. He was shaking an artificial hand.

Sandor nodded, dropped his eyes.

Benedick turned to the big man with the eyepatch. ". . . And you are the Lynx?"

"That is correct, my brother. You must excuse me if I do not shake hands. It is against my religion. I believe that life does not require reassurances as to its oneness."

"Of course," said Benedick. "I once knew a man from Dombeck. He was a *gnil* smuggler, named Worten Wortan—"

"He is gone to join the Great Flame," said the Lynx. "That is to say, he is dead now. ICI apprehended him two years ago. He passed to Flame while attempting to escape restraint."

"Really?" said Benedick. "He was at one time a *gnil* addict himself—"

"I know. I read his file in connection with another case."

"Dombeck is full of *gnil* smugglers"—Sandor.

"Oh. Well, then let us talk of this man Corgo."

"Yes"—the Lynx.

"Yes"—Sandor.

"The ICI man told me that many insurance associations have lodged protests with their Interstel representatives."

"That is true"—Lynx.

"Yes"—Sandor, biting his lip. "Do you gentlemen mind if I remove my legs?"

"Not at all"—the Lynx. "We are coworkers, and informality should govern our gatherings."

"Please do," said Benedick.

Sandor leaned forward in his chair and pressed the

coupling controls. There followed two thumps from beneath his desk. He leaned back then and surveyed his shelves of globes.

"Do they cause you pain?" asked Benedick.

"Yes—" Sandor.

"Were you in an accident?"

"Birth"—Sandor.

The Lynx raised a decanter of brownish liquid to the light. He stared through it.

"It is a local brandy"—Sandor. "Quite good. Somewhat like the *xmili* of Bandla, only nonaddictive. Have some."

The Lynx did, keeping it in front of him all that evening.

"Corgo is a destroyer of property," said Benedick. Sandor nodded.

". . . And a defrauder of insurance associations, a defacer of planetary bodies, a deserter from the Guard—"

"A murderer"—Sandor.

". . . And a zoophilist," finished Benedick.

"Aye"—the Lynx, smacking his lips.

"So great an offender against public tranquility is he that he must be found."

". . . And passed back through the Flame for purification and rebirth."

"Yes, we must locate him and kill him," said Benedick.

"The two pieces of equipment . . . Are they present?"—the Lynx.

"Yes, the phase-wave is in the next room."

". . . And?" asked Benedick.

"The other item is in the bottom drawer of this desk, right side."

"Then why do we not begin now?"

"Yes. Why not now?"—the Lynx.

"Very well"—Sandor. "One of you will have to

open the drawer, though. It is in the brown-glass jar, to the back."

"I'll get it," said Benedick.

A great sob escaped him after a time, as he sat there with rows of worlds at his back, tears on his cheeks, and Corgo's heart clutched in his hands.

"It is cold and dim. . . ."

"Where?"—the Lynx.

"It is a small place. A room? Cabin? Instrument panels . . . A humming sound . . . Cold, and crazy angles everywhere . . . Vibration . . . Hurt!"

"What is he doing?"—Sandor.

". . . Sitting, half-lying—a couch, webbed, about him. Furry one at his side, sleeping. Twisted—angles—everything—wrong. Hurt!"

"The *Wallaby*, in transit"—Lynx.

"Where is he going?"—Sandor.

"HURT!" shouted Benedick.

Sandor dropped the heart into his lap.

He began to shiver. He wiped at his eyes with the backs of his hands.

"I have a headache," he announced.

"Have a drink"—Lynx.

He gulped one, sipped the second.

"Where was I?"

The Lynx raised his shoulders and let them fall.

"The *Wallaby* was fast-phasing somewhere, and Corgo was in phase-sleep. It is a disturbing sensation to fast-phase while fully conscious. Distance and duration grow distorted. You found him at a bad time—while under sedation and subject to continuum-impact. Perhaps tomorrow will be better. . . ."

"I hope so."

"Yes, tomorrow"—Sandor.

"Tomorrow . . . Yes."

"There *was* one other thing," he added, "a thing

in his mind . . . There was a sun where there was no sun before."

"A burn-job?"—Lynx.

"Yes."

"A memory?"—Sandor.

"No. He is on his way to do it."

The Lynx stood.

"I will phase-wave ICI and advise them. They can check which worlds are presently being mined. Have you any ideas how soon?"

"No, I cannot tell that."

"What did the globe look like? What continental configurations?"—Sandor.

"None. The thought was not that specific. His mind was drifting—mainly filled with hate."

"I'll call in now—and we'll try again. . . ?"

"Tomorrow. I'm tired now."

"Go to bed then. Rest."

"Yes, I can do that. . . ."

"Good night, Mister Benedict."

"Good night. . . ."

"Sleep in the heart of the Great Flame."

"I hope not. . . ."

Mala whimpered and moved nearer her Corgo, for she was dreaming an evil dream: they were back on the great snowfield of Brild, and she was trying to help him—to walk, to move forward. He kept slipping through, and lying there longer each time, and rising more slowly each time and moving ahead at an even slower pace, each time. He tried to kindle a fire, but the snow-devils spun and toppled like icicles falling from the seven moons, and the dancing green flames died as soon as they were born from between his hands.

Finally, on the top of a mountain of ice she saw them.

There were three . . .

They were clothed from head to toe in flame; their burning heads turned and turned and turned; and then one bent and sniffed at the ground, rose, and indicated their direction. Then they were racing down the hillside, trailing flames, melting a pathway as they came, springing over drifts and ridges of ice, ther arms extended before them.

Silent they came, pausing only as the one sniffed the air, the ground. . . .

She could hear their breathing now, feel their heat. . . .

In a matter of moments they would arrive. . . .

Mala whimpered and moved nearer her Corgo.

For three days Benedick tried, clutching Corgo's heart like a Gypsy's crystal, watering it with his tears, squeezing it almost to life again. His head ached for hours after, each time that he met the continuum-impact. He wept long, moist tears for hours beyond contact, which was unusual. He had always withdrawn from immediate pain before; remembered distress was his forte, and a different matter altogether.

He hurt each time that he touched Corgo and his mind was sucked down through that subway in the sky; and he touched Corgo eleven times during those three days, and then his power went away, really.

Seated, like a lump of dark metal on the hull of the *Wallaby*, he stared across six hundred miles at the blazing hearth which he had stoked to steel-tempering heights; and he *felt* like a piece of metal, resting there upon an anvil, waiting for the hammer to fall again, as it always did, waiting for it to strike him again and again, and to beat him to a new toughness, to smash away more and more of that within him which was base, of that which knew pity, remorse, and guilt, again and again and again, and to leave only that hard, hard form of hate, like an iron boot, which lived at the core of the lump, himself, and required constant hammering and heat.

Sweating as he watched, smiling, Corgo took pictures.

When one of the nineteen known paranorms in the 149 inhabited worlds in the galaxy suddenly loses his powers, and loses them at a crucial moment, it is like unto the old tales wherein a Princess is stricken one day with an unknown malady and the King, her father, summons all his wise men and calls for the best physicians in the realm.

Big Daddy ICI (*Rex ex machina-like*) did, in similar manner, summon wise men and counselors from various Thinkomats and think-repairshops about the galaxy, including Interstel University, on Earth itself. But alas! While all had a diagnosis none had on hand any suggestions which were immediately acceptable to all parties concerned:

"Bombard his thalamus with Beta particles."

"Hypno-regression to the womb, and restoration at a pre-traumatic point in his life."

"More continuum-impact."

"Six weeks on a pleasure satellite, and two aspirins every four hours."

"There is an old operation called a lobotomy. . . ."

"Lots of liquids and green leafy vegetables."

"Hire another paranorm."

For one reason or another, the principal balked at all of these courses of action, and the final one was impossible at the moment. In the end, the matter was settled neatly by Sandor's nurse, Miss Barbara, who happened onto the veranda one afternoon as Benedick sat there fanning himself and drinking *xmili*.

"Why Mister Benedict!" she announced, plopping her matronly self into the chair opposite him and spiking her *redlonade* with three fingers of *xmili*. "Fancy meeting you out here! I thought you were in the library with the boys, working on that top secret hush-hush critical project called Wallaby Stew, or something."

"As you can see, I am not," he said, staring at his knees.

"Well, it's nice just to pass the time of day sometimes, too. To sit. To relax. To rest from the hunting of Victor Corgo . . ."

"Please, you're not supposed to know about the project. It's top secret and critical—"

"And hush-hush too, I know. Dear Sandor talks in his sleep every night—so much. You see, I tuck him in each evening and sit there until he drifts away to dreamland, poor child."

"Mm, yes. Please don't talk about the project, though."

"Why? Isn't it going well?"

"No!"

"Why not?"

"Because of *me*, if you must know! I've got a block of some kind. The power doesn't come when I call it."

"Oh, how distressing! You mean you can't peep into other persons' minds any more?"

"Exactly."

"Dear me. Well, let's talk about something else then. Did I ever tell you about the days when I was the highest-paid courtesan on Sordido V?"

Benedick's head turned slowly in her direction.

"Nooo . . ." he said. "You mean *the* Sordido?"

"Oh yes. Bright Bad Barby, the Bouncing Baby, they used to call me. They still sing ballads, you know."

"Yes, I've heard them. Many verses . . ."

"Have another drink. I once had a coin struck in my image, you know. It's a collectors' item now, of course. Full-length pose, flesh-colored. Here, I wear it on this chain around my neck—Lean closer, it's a short chain."

"Very—interesting. Uh, how did all this come about?"

"Well—it all began with old Pruria Van Teste, the banker, of the export-import Testes. You see, he had this thing going for synthofemmes for a long while, but when he started getting up there in years he felt there was something he'd been missing. So, one fine day, he sent me ten dozen Hravian orchids and a diamond garter, along with an invitation to have dinner with him. . . ."

"You accepted, of course?"

"Naturally not. Not the first time, anyway. I could see that he was pretty damn eager."

"Well, what happened?"

"Wait till I fix another *redlonade*."

Later that afternoon, the Lynx wandered out into the veranda during the course of his meditations. He saw there Miss Barbara, with Benedick seated beside her, weeping.

"What troubles thy tranquility, my brother?" he inquired.

"Nothing! Nothing at all! It is wonderful and beautiful, everything! My power has come back—I can feel it!" He wiped his eyes on his sleeve.

"Bless thee, little lady!" said the Lynx, seizing Miss Barbara's hand. "Thy simple counsels have done more to heal my brother than have all these highly-paid medical practitioners brought here at great expense. Virtue lies in thy homely words, and thou art most beloved of the Flame."

"Thank you, I'm sure."

"Come brother, let us away to our task again!"

"Yes, let us!—Oh thank you, Bright Barby!"

"Don't mention it"

Benedick's eyes clouded immediately, as he took

the tattered blood-pump into his hands. He leaned back, stroking it, and moist spots formed on either side of his nose, grew like well-fed amoebas, underwent mitosis, and dashed off to explore in the vicinity of his shelf-like upper lip.

He sighed once, deeply.

"Yes, I am there."

He blinked, licked his lips.

". . . It is night. Late. It is a primitive dwelling. Mud-like stucco, bits of straw in it . . . All lights out, but for the one from the machine, and its spillage—"

"Machine?"—Lynx.

"What machine?"—Sandor.

". . . Projector. Pictures on wall . . . World—big, filling whole picture-field—patches of fire on the world, up near the top. Three places—"

"Bhave VII!"—Lynx. "Six days ago!"

"Shoreline to the right goes like this . . . And to the left, like this. . . ."

His right index finger traced patterns in the air.

"Bhave VII"—Sandor.

"Happy and not happy at the same time—hard to separate the two. Guilt, though, is there—but pleasure with it. Revenge . . . Hate people, humans . . . We adjust the projector now, stop it at a flare-up— Bright! How good!—Oh good! That will teach them! —Teach them to grab away what belongs to others . . . To murder a race!—The generator is humming. It is ancient, and it smells bad. . . . The dog is lying on our foot. The foot is asleep, but we do not want to disturb the dog, for it is Mala's favorite thing—her only toy, companion, living doll, four-footed. . . . She is scratching behind its ear with her forelimb, and it loves her. Light leaks down upon them. . . . Clear they are. The breeze is warm, very, which is why we are unshirted. It stirs the tasseled hanging. . . . No force-field or windowpane . . . Insects buzz by the projector—pterodactyl silhouettes on the "burning world—"

"What kind of insects?"—Lynx.

"Can you see what is beyond the window?"—Sandor.

". . . Outside are trees—short ones—just outlines, squat. Can't tell where trunks begin . . . Foliage too thick, too close. Too dark out. Off in the distance a tiny moon . . . Something like *this* on a hill . . ." His hands shaped a turnip impaled on an obelisk. "Not sure how far off, how large, what color, or what made of . . ."

"Is the name of the place in Corgo's mind?"—Lynx.

"If I could touch him, with my hands, I would know it, know everything. Only receive impressions *this* way, though—surface thoughts. He is not thinking of where he is now. . . . The dog rolls onto its back and off of our foot—at last! She scratches its tummy, my love dark . . . It kicks with its hind leg as if scratching after a flea—wags its tail. Dilk is puppy's name. She gave it that name, loves it . . . It is like one of hers. Which was murdered. Hate people—humans. *She* is people. Better than . . . Doesn't butcher that which breathes for selfish gain, for Interstel. Better than people, my pony-friends, better . . . An insect lights on Dilk's nose. She brushes it away. Segmented, two sets of wings, about five millimeters in length, pink globe on front end, bulbous, and buzzes as it goes, the insect—you asked . . ."

"How many entrances are there to the place?" —Lynx.

"Two. One doorway at each end of the hut."

"How many windows?"

"Two. On opposing walls—the ones without doors. I can't see anything through the other window—too dark on that side."

"Anything else?"

"On the wall a sword—long hilt, very long, two-handed—even longer maybe—three? four?—short

blades, though, two of them—hilt is in the middle—
and each blade is straight, double-edged, forearm-
length . . . Beside it, a mask of—flowers? Too dark
to tell. The blades shine; the mask is dull. Looks like
flowers, though. Many little ones . . . Four sides to
the mask, shaped like a kite, big end down. Can't
make out features. It projects fairly far out from the
wall, though. Mala is restless. Probably doesn't like
the pictures—or maybe doesn't see them and is bored.
Her eyes are different. She nuzzles our shoulder
now. We pour her a drink in her bowl. Take another
one ourself. She doesn't drink hers. We stare at her.
She drops her head and drinks. Dirt floor under
our sandals, hard-packed. Many tiny white—pebbles?
—in it, powdery-like. The table is wood, natural . . .
The generator sputters. The picture fades, comes
back. We rub our chin. Need a shave . . . The hell
with it! We're not standing any inspections! Drink—
one, two—all gone! Another!"

Sandor had threaded a tape into his viewer, and
he was spinning it and stopping it, spinning it and
stopping it, spinning it and stopping it. He checked
his worlds chronometer.

"Outside," he asked, "does the moon seem to be
moving up, or down, or across the sky?"

"Across."

"Right to left, or left to right?"

"Right to left. It seems about a quarter past zenith."

"Any coloration to it?"

"Orange, with three black lines. One starts at about
eleven o'clock, crosses a quarter of its surface, drops
straight down, cuts back at seven. The other starts at
two, drops to six. They don't meet. The third is a
small upside-down letter 'c'—lower right quarter . . .
Not big, the moon, but clear, very. No clouds."

"Any constellations you can make out?"—Lynx.

". . . Head isn't turned that way now, wasn't turned

toward the window long enough. Now there is a noise, far off . . . A high-pitched chattering, almost metallic. Animal. He pictures a six-legged tree creature, half the size of a man, reddish-brown hair, sparse . . . It can go on two, four, or six legs on the ground. Doesn't go down on the ground much, though. Nests high. An egg-layer. Many teeth. Eats flesh. Small eyes, and black—two. Great nose-holes. Pesty, but not dangerous to men—easily frightened."

"He is on Disten, the fifth world of Blake's System," said Sandor. "Night-side means he is on the continent Didenlan. The moon Babry, well past zenith now, means he is to the east. A Mellar-mosque indicates a Mella-Muslim settlement. The blade and the mask seem Hortanian. I am sure they were brought from further inland. The chalky deposits would set him in the vicinity of Landear, which *is* Mella-Muslim. It is on the Dista River, north bank. There is much jungle about. Even those people who wish seclusion seldom go further than eight miles from the center of town—population 153,000—and it is least settled to the northwest, because of the hills, the rocks, and—"

"Fine! That's where he is then!"—Lynx. "Now here is how we'll do it. He has, of course, been sentenced to death. I believe—yes, I know!—there is an ICI Field Office on the second world—whatever its name—of that System."

"Nirer"—Sandor.

"Yes. Hmm, let's see . . . Two agents will be empowered as executioners. They will land their ship to the northwest of Landear, enter the city, and find where the man with the strange four-legged pet settled, the one who arrived within the past six days. Then one agent will enter the hut and ascertain whether Corgo is within. He will retreat immediately if Corgo is present, signaling to the other who will be hidden behind those trees or whatever. The second man will then fire a round of fragmentation plaster through the unguarded window. One agent will then position himself at a safe distance beyond the northeast corner of the edifice, so as to cover a door and a window. The other will move to the southwest, to do the same. Each will carry a two-hundred channel laser sub-gun with vibrating head. —Good! I'll phase-wase it to Central now. We've got him!"

He hurried from the room.

Benedick, still holding the thing, his shirt-front soaking, continued:

" 'Fear not, my lady dark. He is but a puppy, and he howls at the moon. . . .' "

It was thirty-one hours and twenty minutes later when the Lynx received and decoded the two terse statements:

EXECUTIONERS THE WAY OF ALL FLESH.
THE WALLABY HAS JUMPED AGAIN.

He licked his lips. His comrades were waiting for the report, and *they* had succeeded—they had done their part, had performed efficiently and well. It was the Lynx who had missed his kill.

He made the sign of the Flame and entered the library.

Benedick knew—*he* could tell. The little paranorm's hands were on his walking stick, and that was enough—just that.

The Lynx bowed his head.

"We begin again," he told them.

Benedick's powers—if anything, stronger than ever—survived continuum-impact seven more times. Then he described a new world: big it was, and many-peopled—bright—dazzling, under a blue-white sun; yellow brick everywhere, neo-Denebian architecture, green glass windows, a purple sea nearby. . . .

No trick at all for Sandor:

"Phillip's World," he named it, then told them the city: "Delles."

"This time *we* burn *him*," said the Lynx, and he was gone from the room.

"Christian-Zoroastrians," sighed Benedick, after he had left. "I think this one has a Flame-complex."

Sandor spun the globe with his left hand and watched it turn.

"I'm not preconning," said Benedick, "but I'll give you odds, like three to one—on Corgo's escaping again."

"Why?"

"When he abandoned humanity he became something less, and more. He is not ready to die."

"What do you mean?"

"I hold his heart. He gave it up, in all ways. He is invincible now. But he will reclaim it one day. Then he will die."

"How do you know?"

". . . A feeling. There are many types of doctors, among them pathologists. No less than others, they; but masters only of blackness. I *know* people, have known many. I do not pretend to know *all* about them. But weaknesses—yes, those I know."

Sandor turned his globe and did not say anything.

But they *did* burn the *Wallaby*, badly.

He lived, though.

He lived, cursing.

As he lay there in the gutter, the world burning, exploding, falling down around him, he cursed *that* world and every other, and everything in them.

Then there was another burst.

Blackness followed.

* * *

The double-bladed Hortanian sword, spinning in the hands of Corgo, had halved the first ICI executioner as he stood in the doorway. Mala had detected their approach across the breezes, through the open window.

The second had fallen before the fragmentation plaster could be launched. Corgo had a laser sub-gun himself, Guard issue, and he cut the man down, firing through the wall and two trees in the direction Mala indicated.

Then the *Wallaby* left Disten.

But he was troubled. How had they found him so quickly? He had had close brushes with them before—many of them, over the years. But he was cautious, and he could not see where he had failed this time, could not understand how Interstel had located him. Even his last employer did not know his whereabouts.

He shook his head and phased for Phillip's World.

To die is to sleep and not to dream, and Corgo did not want this. He took elaborate pains, in-phasing and out-phasing in random directions; he gave Mala a golden collar with a two-way radio in its clasp, wore its mate within his death-ring; he converted much currency, left the *Wallaby* in the care of a reputable smuggler in Unassociated Territory and crossed Phillip's World to Delles-by-the-Sea. He was fond of sailing, and he liked the purple waters of this planet. He rented a large villa near the Delles Dives—slums to the one side, Riviera to the other. This pleased him. He still had dreams; he was not dead yet.

Sleeping, perhaps, he had heard a sound. Then he was suddenly seated on the side of his bed, a handful of death in his hand.

"Mala?"

She was gone. The sound he'd heard had been the closing of a door.

He activated the radio.

"What is it?" he demanded.

"I have the feeling we are watched again," she replied, through his ring. ". . . Only a feeling, though."

Her voice was distant, tiny.

"Why did you not tell *me*? Come back—now."

"No. I match the night and can move without sound. I will investigate. There *is* something, if I have fear. . . . Arm yourself!"

He did that, and as he moved toward the front of the house they struck. He ran. As he passed through the front door they struck again, and again. There was an inferno at his back, and a steady rain of plaster, metal, wood and glass was falling. Then there was an inferno around him.

They were above him. This time they had been cautioned not to close with him, but to strike from a distance. This time they hovered high in a shielded globe and poured down hot rivers of destruction.

Something struck him in the head and the shoulder. He fell, turning. He was struck in the chest, the stomach. He covered his face and rolled, tried to rise, failed. He was lost in a forest of flames. He got into a crouch, ran, fell again, rose once more, ran, fell again, crawled, fell again.

As he lay there in the gutter, the world burning, exploding, falling down around him he cursed *that* world and every other, and everyone in them.

Then there was another burst.

Blackness followed.

They thought they had succeeded, and their joy was great.

"Nothing," Benedick had said, smiling through his tears.

So that day they celebrated, and the next.

But Corgo's body had not been recovered.

Almost half a block had been hurled down, though, and eleven other residents could not be located either, so it seemed safe to assume that the execution had succeeded. ICI, however, requested that the trio remain together on Dombeck for another ten days, while further investigations were carried out.

Benedick laughed.

"Nothing," he repeated. "Nothing."

But there is a funny thing about a man without a heart: his body does not live by the same rules as those of others: no. The egg in his chest is smarter than a mere heart, and it is the center of a wonderful communications system. Dead itself, it is omniscient in terms of that which lives around it; it is not omnipotent, but it has resources which a living heart does not command.

As the burns and laceratons were flashed upon the screen of the body, it sat in instant criticism. It moved itself to an emergency level of function; it became a flag vibrating within a hurricane; the glands responded and poured forth their juices of power; muscles were activated as if by electricity.

Corgo was only half-aware of the inhuman speed with which he moved through the storm of heat and the hail of building materials. It tore at him, but this pain was canceled. His massive output jammed non-essential neural input. He made it as far as the street and collapsed in the shelter of the curb.

The egg took stock of the cost of the action, decided the price had been excessively high, and employed immediate measures to insure the investment.

Down, down did it send him. Into the depths of sub-coma. Standard-model humans cannot decide one day that they wish to hibernate, lie down, do it. The physicians can induce *dauersch-laff* with combinations of drugs and elaborate machineries. But Corgo did not need these things. He had a built-in survival kit with a mind of its own; and it decided that he must go deeper than the mere coma-level that a heart would have permitted. So it did the things a heart cannot do, while maintaining its own functions.

It hurled him into the blackness of sleep without dreams, of total unawareness. For only at the border of death itself could his life be retained, be strengthened, grow again. To approach this near the realm of death, its semblance was necessary.

Therefore, Corgo lay dead in the gutter.

People, of course, flock to the scene of any disaster.

Those from the Riviera pause to dress in their best catastrophe clothing. Those from the slums do not, because their wardrobes are not as extensive.

One though, was dressed already and was passing nearby. "Zim" was what he was called, for obvious reasons. He had had another name once, but he had all but forgotten it.

He was staggering home from the *zimlak* parlor where he had cashed his Guard pension check for that month-cycle.

There was an explosion, but it was seconds before he realized it. Muttering, he stopped and turned very slowly in the direction of the noise. Then he saw the flames. He looked up, saw the hoverglobe. A memory appeared within his mind and he winced and continued to watch.

After a time he saw the man, moving at a fantastic pace across the landscape of Hell. The man fell in the street. There was more burning, and then the globe departed.

The impressions finally registered, and his disaster-reflex made him approach.

Indelible synapses, burnt into his brain long ago, summoned up page after page of The Complete Guard Field Manual of Immediate Medical Actions. He knelt beside the body, red with burn, blood and firelight.

". . . Captain," he said, as he stared into the angular face with the closed dark eyes. "Captain . . ."

He covered his own face with his hands and they came away wet.

"Neighbors. Here. Us. Didn't—know . . ." He listened for a heartbeat, but there was nothing that he could detect. "Fallen . . . On the deck my Captain lies . . . Fallen . . . cold . . . dead. Us. Neighbors, even . . ." His sob was a jagged thing, until he was seized with a spell of hiccups. Then he steadied his hands and raised an eyelid.

Corgo's head jerked two inches to his left, away from the brightness of the flames.

The man laughed in relief.

"You're alive, Cap! You're still alive!"

The thing that was Corgo did not reply.

Bending, straining, he raised the body.

" 'Do not move the victim'—that's what it says in the Manual. But you're coming with me, Cap. I remember now . . . It was after I left. But I remember . . . All. Now I remember; I do . . . Yes. They'll kill you another time—if you do live. . . . They will; I know. So I'll have to move the victim. Have to . . . —Wish I wasn't so fogged . . . I'm sorry, Cap. You were always good, to the men, good to me. Ran a tight ship, but you were good . . . Old *Wallaby*, happy . . . Yes. We'll go now, killer. Fast as we can. Before the Morbs come—yes. I remember . . . you. Good man, Cap. Yes."

So, the *Wallaby* had made its last jump, according to the ICI investigation which followed. But Corgo still dwelled on the dreamless border, and the seeds and the egg held his life.

After the ten days had passed, the Lynx and Benedick still remained with Sandor. Sandor was not anxious for them to go. He had never been employed before; he liked the feeling of having coworkers about, persons who shared memories of things done. Benedick was loathe to leave Miss Barbara, one of the few persons he could talk to and have answer him, willingly. The Lynx liked the food and the climate, decided his wives and grandchildren could use a vacation.

So they stayed on.

Returning from death is a deadly slow business. Reality does the dance of the veils, and it is a long while before you know what lies beneath them all (if you ever really do).

When Corgo had formed a rough idea, he cried out: "Mala!"

. . . The darkness.

Then he saw a face out of times gone by.

"Sergeant Emil . . . ?"

"Yes, sir. Right here, Captain."

"Where am I?"

"My hutch, sir. Yours got burnt out."

"How?"

"A hoverglobe did it, with a sear-beam."

"What of my—pet? A Drillen . . ."

"There was only you I found, sir—no one, nothing, else. Uh, it was almost a month-cycle ago that it happened. . . ."

Corgo tried to sit up, failed, tried again, half-succeeded. He sat propped on his elbows.

"What's the matter with me?"

"You had some fractures, burns, lacerations, internal injuries—but you're going to be all right, now."

"I wonder how they found me, so fast—again . . . ?"

"I don't know, sir. Would you like to try some broth now?"

"Later."

"It's all warm and ready."

"Okay, Emil. Sure, bring it on."

He lay back and wondered.

There was her voice. He had been dozing all day and he was part of a dream.

"Corgo, are you there? Are you there, Corgo? Are you . . ."

His hand! The ring!

"Yes! Me! Corgo!" He activated it. "Mala! Where are you?"

"In a cave, by the sea. Everyday I have called to you. Are you alive, or do you answer me from Elsewhere?"

"I am alive. There is no magic to your collar. How have you kept yourself?"

"I go out at night. Steal food from the large dwellings with the green windows like doors—for Dilk and myself."

"The puppy? Alive, too?"

"Yes. He was penned in the yard on that night. . . . Where are you?"

"I do not know, precisely. . . . Near where our place was. A few blocks away—I'm with an old friend. . . ."

"I must come."

"Wait until dark. I'll get you directions—no. I'll send him after you, my friend. . . . Where is your cave?"

"Up the beach, past the red house you said was ugly. There are three rocks, pointed on top. Past them is a narrow path—the water comes up to it, sometimes covers it—and around a corner then, thirty-one of my steps, and the rock hangs overhead, too. It goes far back then, and there is a crack in the wall—small enough to squeeze through, but it widens. We are here."

"My friend will come for you after dark."

"You are hurt?"

"I was. But I am better now. I'll see you later, talk more then."

"Yes—"

In the days that followed, his strength returned to him. He played chess with Emil and talked with him of their days together in the Guard. He laughed, for the first time in many years, at the tale of the Commander's wig, at the Big Brawl on Sordido III, some thirty-odd years before. . . .

Mala kept to herself, and to Dilk. Occasionally, Corgo would feel her eyes upon him. But whenever he turned, she was always looking in another direction. He realized that she had never seen him being friendly with anyone before. She seemed puzzled.

He drank *zimlak* with Emil, they ventured off-key ballads together. . . .

Then one day it struck him.

"Emil, what are you using for money these days?"

"Guard pension, Cap."

"Flames! We've been eating you out of business! Food, and the medical supplies and all . . ."

"I had a little put away for foul weather days, Cap."

"Good. But you shouldn't have been using it. There's quite a bit of money zipped up in my boots. Here. Just a second . . . There! Take these!"

"I can't, Cap. . . ."

"The hell, you say! Take them, that's an order!"

"All right, sir, but you don't have to. . . ."

"Emil, there is a price on my head—you know?"

"I know."

"A pretty large reward."

"Yes."

"It's yours, by right."

"I couldn't turn you in, sir."

"Nevertheless, the reward is yours. Twice over. I'll send you that amount—a few weeks after I leave here."

"I couldn't take it, sir."

"Nonsense; you will."

"No, sir. I won't."

"What do you mean?"

"I just mean I couldn't take that money."

"Why not? What's wrong with it?"

"Nothing, exactly . . . I just don't want any of it. I'll take this you gave me for the food and stuff. But no more, that's all."

"Oh . . . All right, Emil. Any way you like it. I wasn't trying to force . . ."

"I know, Cap."

"Another game now? I'll spot you a bishop and three pawns this time."

"Very good, sir."

"We had some good times together, eh?"

"You bet, Cap. Tau Ceti—three months' leave. Remember the Red River Valley—and the family of native life-forms?"

"Hah! And Cygnus VII—the purple world with the Rainbow Women?"

"Took me three weeks to get that dye off me. Thought at first it was a new disease. Flames! I'd love to ship out again!"

Corgo paused in midmove.

"Hmm . . . You know, Emil . . . It might be that you could."

"What do you mean?"

Corgo finished his move.

"Aboard the *Wallaby*. It's here, in Unassociated Territory, waiting for me. I'm Captain, and crew—and everything—all by myself, right now. Mala helps some, but—you know, I could use a First Mate. Be like old times."

Emil replaced the knight he had raised, looked up, looked back down.

"I—I don't know what to say, Cap. I never thought you'd offer me a berth. . . ."

"Why not? I could use a good man. Lots of action,

like the old days. Plenty of cash. No cares. We want three months' leave on Tau Ceti and we write our own bloody orders. We take it!"

"I—I do want to space again, Cap—bad. But—no, I couldn't. . . ."

"Why not, Emil? Why not? It'd be just like before."

"I don't know how to say it, Cap. . . . But when we—burnt places, before—well, it was criminals—pirates, Code-breakers—you know. Now . . . Well, now I hear you burn—just people. Uh, non-Code-breakers. Like, just plain civilians. Well—I could not."

Corgo did not answer. Emil moved his knight.

"I hate them, Emil," he said, after a time. "Every lovin' one of them, I hate them. Do you know what they did on Brild? To the Drillen?"

"Yessir. But it wasn't civilians, and not the miners. It was not *everybody*. It wasn't every lovin' one of them, sir—I just couldn't. Don't be mad."

"I'm not mad, Emil."

"I mean, sir, there are some as I wouldn't mind burnin', Code or no Code. But not the way you do it, sir. And I'd do it for free to those as have it coming."

"Huh!"

Corgo moved his one bishop.

"That's why my money is no good with you?"

"No, sir. That's not it, sir. Well maybe part . . . But only part. I just couldn't take pay for helping someone I—respected, admired."

"You use the past tense."

"Yessir. But I still think you got a raw deal, and what they did to the Drillen was wrong and bad and—evil—but you can't hate everybody for that, sir, because *everybody* didn't do it."

"They countenanced it, Emil—which is just as bad. I am able to hate them all for that alone. And people are all alike, all the same. I burn without discrimination these days, because it doesn't really matter *who*. The guilt is equally distributed. Mankind is commonly culpable."

"No, sir, begging your pardon, sir, but in a system as big as Interstel not everybody knows what everybody else is up to. There are those feeling the same way you do, and there are those as don't give a damn, and those who just don't know a lot of what's going on, but who would do something about it if they knew, soon enough."

"It's your move, Emil."

"Yessir."

"You know, I wish you'd accepted a commission, Emil. You had the chance. You'd have been a good officer."

"No, sir. I'd not have been a good officer. I'm too easygoing. The men would've walked all over me."

"It's a pity. But it's always that way. You know? The good ones are too weak, too easygoing. Why is that?"

"Dunno, sir."

After a couple of moves:

"You know, if I were to give it up—the burning, I mean—and just do some ordinary, decent smuggling with the *Wallaby*, it would be okay. With me. Now. I'm tired. I'm so damned tired I'd just like to sleep—oh, four, five, six years, I think. Supposing I stopped the burning and just shipped stuff here and there—would you sign on with me then?"

"I'd have to think about it, Cap."

"Do that, then. Please. I'd like to have you along."

"Yessir. Your move, sir."

It would not have happened that he'd have been found by his actions, because he *did* stop the burning; it would not have happened—because he was dead on ICI's books—that anyone would have been looking for him. It happened, though—because of a surfeit of *xmili* and goodwill on the part of the hunters.

On the eve of the breaking of the fellowship, nostalgia followed high spirits.

Benedick had never had a friend before, you must remember. Now he had three, and he was leaving them.

The Lynx had ingested much good food and drink, and the good company of simple, maimed people, whose neuroses were unvitiated with normal sophistication—and he had enjoyed this.

Sandor's sphere of human relations had been expanded by approximately a third, and he had slowly come to consider himself at least an honorary member of the vast flux which he had only known before as humanity, or Others.

So, in the library, drinking, and eating and talking, they returned to the hunt. Dead tigers are always the best kind.

Of course, it wasn't long before Benedick picked up the heart, and held it as a connoisseur would an art object—gently, and with a certain mingling of awe and affection.

As they sat there, an odd sensation crept into the pudgy paranorm's stomach and rose slowly, like gas, until his eyes burned.

"I—I'm reading," he said.

"Of course"—the Lynx.

"Yes"—Sandor.

"Really!"

"Naturally"—the Lynx. "He is on Disten, fifth world of Blake's System, in a native hut outside Landear—"

"No"—Sandor. "He is on Phillip's World, in Delles-by-the-Sea."

They laughed, the Lynx a deep rumble, Sandor a gasping chuckle.

"No," said Benedick. "He is in transit, aboard

the *Wallaby*. He had just phased and his mind is still mainly awake. He is running a cargo of ambergris to the Tau Ceti system, fifth planet—Tholmen. After that he plans on vacationing in the Red River Valley of the third planet—Cardiff. Along with the Drillen and the puppy, he has a crewman with him this time. I can't read anything but that it's a retired Guardsman."

"By the holy Light of the Great and Glorious Flame!"

"We know they never did find his ship. . . ."

". . . And his body was not recovered. Could *you* be mistaken, Benedick? Reading something, someone else . . . ?"

"No."

"What should we do, Lynx?"—Sandor.

"An unethical person might be inclined to forget it. It is a closed case. We *have* been paid and dismissed."

"True."

"But think of when he strikes again. . . ."

". . . It would be because of us, our failure."

"Yes."

". . . And many would die."

". . . And much machinery destroyed, and an insurance association defrauded."

"Yes."

". . . Because of us."

"Yes."

"So we should report it"—Lynx.

"Yes."

"It is unfortunate. . . ."

"Yes."

". . . But it will be good to have worked together this final time."

"Yes. It will. Very."

"Tholmen, in Tau Ceti, and he just phased?"—Lynx.

"Yes."

"I'll call, and they'll be waiting for him in T.C."

". . . I told you," said the weeping paranorm. "He wasn't ready to die."

Sandor smiled and raised his glass with his flesh-colored hand.

There was still some work to be done.

When the *Wallaby* hit Tau Ceti all hell broke loose.

Three fully-manned Guardships, like unto the *Wallaby* herself, were waiting.

ICI had quarantined the entire system for three days. There could be no mistaking the ebony toadstool when it appeared on the screen. No identification was solicited.

The tractor beams missed it the first time, however, and the *Wallaby*'s new First Mate fired every weapon aboard the ship simultaneously, in all directions, as soon as the alarm sounded. This had been one of Corgo's small alterations in fire-control, because of the size of his operations: no safety circuits; and it was a suicide-ship, if necessary: it was a lone wolf with no regard for *any* pack: one central control—touch it, and the *Wallaby* became a porcupine with laser-quills, stabbing into anything in every direction.

Corgo prepared to phase again, but it took him forty-three seconds to do so.

During that time he was struck twice by the surviving Guardship.

Then he was gone.

Time and Chance, which govern all things, and sometimes like to pass themselves off as Destiny, then seized upon the *Wallaby*, the puppy, the Drillen, First Mate Emil, and the man without a heart.

Corgo had set no course when he had in-phased. There had been no time.

The two blasts from the Guardship had radically

altered the *Wallaby*'s course, and had burnt out twenty-three fast-phase projectors.

The *Wallaby* jumped blind, and with a broken leg.

Continuum-impact racked the crew. The hull repaired rents in its skin.

They continued for thirty-nine hours and twenty-three minutes, taking turns at sedation, watching for the first warning on the panel.

The *Wallaby* held together, though.

But where they had gotten to no one knew, least of all a weeping paranorm who had monitored the battle and all of Corgo's watches, despite the continuum-impact and a hangover.

But suddenly Benedick knew fear:

"He's about to phase-out. I'm going to have to drop him now."

"Why?"—the Lynx.

"Do you know where he is?"

"No, of course not!"

"Well, neither does he. Suppose he pops out in the middle of a sun, or in some atmosphere—moving at that speed?"

"Well, supposing he does? He dies."

"Exactly. Continuum-impact is bad enough. I've never been in a man's mind when he died—and I don't think I could take it. Sorry. I just won't do it. I think I might die myself if it happened. I'm so tired now. . . . I'll just have to check him out later."

With that he collapsed and could not be roused.

So, Corgo's heart went back into its jar, and the jar went back into the lower right-hand drawer of Sandor's desk, and none of the hunters heard the words of Corgo's answer to his First Mate after the phasing-out:

"Where are we?—The Comp says the nearest thing is a little ping-pong ball of a world called Dombeck, not noted for anything. We'll have to put down there for repairs, somewhere off the beaten track. We need projectors."

So they landed the *Wallaby* and banged on its hull as the hunters slept, some 542 miles away.

They were grinding out the projector sockets shortly after Sandor had been tucked into his bed.

They reinforced the hull in three places while the Lynx ate half a ham, three biscuits, two apples and a pear, and drank half a liter of Dombeck's best Mosel.

They rewired shorted circuits as Benedick smiled and dreamt of Bright Bad Barby the Bouncing Baby, in the days of her youth.

And Corgo took the light-boat and headed for a town three hundred miles away, just as the pale sun of Dombeck began to rise.

"He's here!" cried Benedick, flinging wide the door to the Lynx's room and rushing up to the bedside. "He's—"

Then he was unconscious, for the Lynx may not be approached suddenly as he sleeps.

When he awakened five minutes later, he was lying on the bed and the entire household stood about him. There was a cold cloth on his forehead and his throat felt crushed.

"My brother," said the Lynx, "you should never approach a sleeping man in such a manner."

"B-but he's here," said Benedick, gagging. "Here on Dombeck! I don't even need Sandor to tell!"

"Art sure thou hast not imbibed too much?"

"No, I tell you he's here!" He sat up, flung away the cloth. "That little city, Coldstream—" He pointed through the wall. "—I was there just a week ago. I *know* the place!"

"You have had a dream—"

"Wet your Flame! But I've not! I held his heart in these hands and saw it!"

The Lynx winced at the profanity, but considered the possibility.

"Then come with us to the library and see if you can read it again."

"You better believe I can!"

At that moment Corgo was drinking a cup of coffee and waiting for the town to wake up. He was considering his First Mate's resignation:

"I never wanted to burn anyone, Cap. Least of all, the Guard. I'm sorry, but that's it. No more for me. Leave me here and give me passage home to Phillip's —that's all I want. I know you didn't want it the way it happened, but if I keep shipping with you it might happen again some day. Probably will. They got your number somehow, and I couldn't *ever* do *that* again. I'll help you fix the *Wallaby*, then I'm out. Sorry."

Corgo sighed and ordered a second coffee. He glanced at the clock on the diner wall. Soon, soon . . .

"That clock, that wall, that window! It's the diner where I had lunch last week, in Coldstream!" said Benedick, blinking moistly.

"Do you think all that continuum-impact . . . ?" —the Lynx.

"I don't know"—Sandor.

"How can we check?"

"Call the flamin' diner and ask them to describe their only customer!"—Benedick.

"*That* is a very good idea"—the Lynx.

The Lynx moved to the phone-unit on Sandor's desk.

Sudden, as everything concerning the case had been, was the Lynx's final decision:

"Your flyer, brother Sandor. May I borrow it?"

"Why, yes. Surely . . ."

"I will now call the local ICI office and requisition a laser-cannon. They have been ordered to cooperate with us without question, and the orders are still in effect. My executioner's rating has never been suspended. It appears that if we ever want to see this job completed we must do it ourselves. It won't take long to mount the gun on your flyer. Benedick, stay with him every minute now. He still has to buy the equipment, take it back, and install it. Therefore, we should have sufficient time. Just stay with him and advise me as to his movements."

"Check."

"Are you sure it's the right way to go about it?" —Sandor.

"I'm sure. . . ."

As the cannon was being delivered, Corgo made his purchases. As it was being installed, he loaded the light-boat and departed. As it was tested, on a tree stump Aunt Faye had wanted removed for a long while, he was aloft and heading toward the desert.

As he crossed the desert, Benedick watched the rolling dunes, scrub-shrubs and darting *rabbophers* through his eyes.

He also watched the instrument panel.

As the Lynx began his journey, Mala and Dilk were walking about the hull of the *Wallaby*. Mala wondered if the killing was over. She was not sure she liked the new Corgo so much as she did the avenger. She wondered whether the change would be permanent. She hoped not. . . .

The Lynx maintained radio contact with Benedick.

Sandor drank *xmili* and smiled.

After a time, Corgo landed.

The Lynx was racing across the sands from the opposite direction.

They began unloading the light-boat.

The Lynx sped on.

"I am near it now. Five minutes," he radioed back.

"Then I'm out?"—Benedick.

"Not yet"—the reply.

"Sorry, but you know what I said. I won't be there when he dies."

"All right, I can take it from here"—the Lynx.

Which is how, when the Lynx came upon the scene, he saw a dog and a man and an ugly but intelligent quadruped beside the *Wallaby*.

His first blast hit the ship. The man fell.

The quadruped ran, and he burnt it.

The dog dashed through the port into the ship.

The Lynx brought the flyer about for another pass.

There was another man, circling around from the other side of the ship, where he had been working.

The man raised his hand and there was a flash of light.

Corgo's death-ring discharged its single laser beam.

It crossed the distance between them, penetrated the hull of the flyer, passed through the Lynx's left arm above the elbow, and continued on through the roof of the vehicle.

The Lynx cried out, fought the controls, as Corgo dashed into the *Wallaby*.

Then he triggered the cannon, and again, and again and again, circling, until the *Wallaby* was a smoldering ruin in the middle of a sea of fused sand.

Still did he burn that ruin, finally calling back to Benedick Benedict and asking his one question.

"Nothing"—the reply.

Then he turned and headed back, setting the autopilot and opening the first-aid kit.

". . . Then he went in to hit the *Wallaby*'s guns, but I hit him first"—Lynx.

"No"—Benedick.

"What meanest thou 'no'? *I* was there."

"So was I, for awhile. I *had* to see how he felt."

"And?"

"He went in for the puppy, Dilk, held it in his arms, and said to it, 'I am sorry.'"

"Whatever, he is dead now and we have finished. It is over"—Sandor.

"Yes."

"Yes."

"Let us then drink to a job well done, before we part for good."

"Yes."

"Yes."

And they did.

While there wasn't much left of the *Wallaby* or its Captain, ICI positively identified a synthetic heart found still beating, erratically, amidst the hot wreckage.

Corgo was dead, and that was it.

He should have known what he was up against, and turned himself in to the proper authorities. How can you hope to beat a man who can pick the lock to your mind, a man who dispatched forty-eight men and seventeen malicious alien life-forms, and a man who knows every damn street in the galaxy?

He should have known better than to go up against Sandor Sandor, Benedick Benedict and Lynx Links. He should, he should have known.

For their real names, of course, are Tisiphone, Alecto and Maegaera. They are the Furies. They arise from chaos and deliver revenge; they convey confusion and disaster to those who abandon the law and forsake the way, who offend against the light and violate the life, who take the power of Flame, like a lightning rod in their two too mortal hands.

THE GRAVEYARD HEART

They were dancing.

—at the party of the century, the party of the millenium, and the Party of Parties,

—really, as well as calendar-wise,

—and he wanted to crush her, to tear her to pieces. . . .

Moore did not really see the pavilion through which they moved, nor regard the hundred faceless shadows that glided about them. He did not take particular note of the swimming globes of colored light that followed above and behind them.

He felt these things, but he did not necessarily sniff wilderness in that ever-green relic of Christmaspast turning on its bright pedestal in the center of the room—shedding its fireproofed needles and traditions these six days after the fact.

All of these were abstracted and dismissed, inhaled and filed away. . . .

In a few more moments it would be Two Thousand.

Leota (nee Lilith) rested in the bow of his arm like a quivering arrow, until he wanted to break her or send her flying (he knew not where), to crush her into limpness, to make that samadhi, myopia, or whatever, go away from her gray-green eyes. At about that time, each time, she would lean against him and whisper something into his ear, something in French, a language he did not yet speak. She followed his inept lead so perfectly though, that it was not unwarranted that he should feel she could read his mind by pure kinesthesia.

Which made it all the worse then, whenever her breath collared his neck with a moist warmness that spread down under his jacket like an invisible infection. Then he would mutter, "C'est vrai" or "Damn" or both and try to crush her bridal whiteness (overlaid with black webbing), and she would become an arrow once more. But she was dancing with him, which was a decided improvement over his last year/her yesterday.

It was almost Two Thousand.

Now . . .

The music broke itself apart and grew back together again as the globes blared daylight. Auld acquaintance, he was reminded, was not a thing to be trifled with.

He almost chuckled then, but the lights went out a moment later and he found himself occupied.

A voice speaking right beside him, beside everyone, stated:

"It is now Two Thousand. Happy New Year!"

He crushed her.

No one cared about Times Square. The crowds in the Square had been watching a relay of the Party on a jerry-screen the size of a football field. Even now the onlookers were being amused by blacklight close-ups of the couples on the dance floor. Perhaps at that very moment, Moore decided, they themselves were the subject of a hilarious sequence being served up before that overflowing petri dish across the ocean. It was quite likely, considering his partner.

He did not care if they laughed at him, though. He had come too far to care.

"I love you," he said silently. (He used mental dittos to presume an answer, and this made him feel somewhat happier.) Then the lights fireflied once more and auld acquaintance was remembered. A blizzard compounded of a hundred smashed rainbows began falling about the couples; slow-melting spirals of confetti drifted through the lights, dissolving as they descended upon the dancers; furry-edged projections of Chinese dragon kites swam overhead, grinning their way through the storm.

They resumed dancing and he asked her the same question he had asked her the year before.

"Can't we be alone, together, somewhere, just for a moment?"

She smothered a yawn.

"No, I'm bored. I'm going to leave in half an hour."

If voices can be throaty and rich, hers was an opulent neckful. Her throat *was* golden, to a well-sunned turn.

"Then let's spend it talking—in one of the little dining rooms."

"Thank you, but I'm not hungry. I *must* be seen for the next half hour."

Primitive Moore, who had spent most of his life dozing at the back of Civilized Moore's brain, rose to his haunches then, with a growl. Civilized Moore muzzled him though, because he did not wish to spoil things.

"When can I see you again?" he asked grimly.

"Perhaps Bastille Day," she whispered. "There's the Liberté, Égalité, Fraternité Fête Nue . . ."

"Where?"

"In the New Versailles Dome, at nine. If you'd like an invitation, I'll see that you receive one. . . ."

"Yes, I do want one."

("She made you ask," jeered Primitive Moore.)

"Very well, you'll receive one in May."

"Won't you spare me a day or so now?"

She shook her head, her blue-blonde coif burning his face.

"Time is too dear," she whispered in mock-Camille pathos, "and the days of the Parties are without end. You ask me to cut years off my life and hand them to you."

"That's right."

"You ask too much," she smiled.

He wanted to curse her right then and walk away, but he wanted even more so to stay with her. He was twenty-seven, an age of which he did not approve in the first place, and he had spent all of the year 1999 wanting her. He had decided two years ago that he was going to fall in love and marry— because he could finally afford to do so without altering his standards of living. Lacking a woman who combined the better qualities of Aphrodite and a digital computer, he had spent an entire year on safari, trekking after the spoor of his starcrossed.

The invitation to the Bledsoes' Orbiting New Year— which had hounded the old year around the world, chasing it over the International Dateline and off the Earth entirely, to wherever old years go—had set him back a month's pay, but had given him his first live glimpse of Leota Mathilde Mason, belle of the Sleepers. Forgetting about digital computers, he decided then and there to fall in love with her. He was old-fashioned in many respects.

He had spoken with her for precisely ninety-seven seconds, the first twenty of which had been Arctic. But he realized that she existed to be admired, so he insisted on admiring her. Finally, she consented to be seen dancing with him at the Millenium Party in Stockholm.

He had spent the following year anticipating her seduction back to a reasonable and human mode of existence. Now, in the most beautiful city in the world, she had just informed him that she was bored and was about to retire until Bastille Day. It was then that Primitive Moore realized what Civilized Moore must really have known all along: the next time that he saw her she would be approximately two days older and he would be going on twenty-nine. Time stands still for the Set, but the price of mortal existence is age. Money could buy her the most desirable of all narcissist indulgences: the cold-bunk.

And he had not even had the chance of a Stockholm snowflake in the Congo to speak with her, to speak more than a few disjointed sentences, let alone to try talking her out of the ice-box club. (Even now, Setman laureate Wayne Unger was moving to cut in on him, with the expression of a golf pro about to give a lesson.)

"Hello, Leota. Sorry, Mister Uh."

Primitive Moore snarled and bashed him with his club; Civilized Moore released one of the most inaccessible women in the world to a god of the Set.

She was smiling. He was smiling. They were gone.

All the way around the world to San Francisco, sitting in the bar of the stratocruiser in the year of Our Lord Two Thousand—that is to say: two, zero, zero, zero—Moore felt that Time was out of joint.

It was two days before he made up his mind what he was going to do about it.

He asked himself (from the blister balcony of his suite in the Hundred Towers of the Hilton-Frisco Complex): *Is this the girl I want to marry?*

He answered himself (looking alternately at the traffic capillaries below his shoetops and the Bay): Yes.

Why? he wanted to know.

Because she is beautiful, he answered, and the future will be lovely. I want her for my beautiful wife in the lovely future.

So he decided to join the Set.

He realized it was no mean feat he was mapping out. First, he required money, lots of money—green acres of Presidents, to be strewn properly in the proper places. The next requisite was distinction, recognition. Unfortunately, the world was full of electrical engineers, humming through their twenty-hour weeks, dallying with pet projects—competent, capable, even inspired—who did not have these things. So he knew it would be difficult.

He submerged himself into research with a unique will: forty, sixty, eighty hours a week he spent—reading, designing, studying taped courses in subjects he had never needed. He gave up on recreation.

By May, when he received his invitation, he stared at the engraved (not fac-copy) parchment (not jot-sheet) with bleary eyes. He had already had nine patents entered and three more were pending. He had sold one and was negotiating with Akwa Mining over a water purification process which he had, he felt, fallen into. Money he would have, he decided, if he could keep up the pace.

Possibly even some recognition. That part now depended mainly on his puro-process and what he did with the money. Leota (nee Lorelei) lurked beneath his pages of formulas, was cubed Braque-like in the lines on his sketcher; she burnt as he slept, slept as he burned.

In June he decided he needed a rest.

"Assistant Division Chief Moore," he told the face in the groomer (his laudatory attitude toward work had already earned him a promotion at the Seal-Lock Division of Pressure Units, Corporate), "you need more French and better dancing."

The groomer hands patted away at his sandy stubble and slashed smooth the shagginess above his ears. The weary eyes before him agreed bluely; they were tired of studying abstractions.

The intensity of his recreation, however, was as fatiguing in its own way as his work had been. His muscle tone *did* improve as he sprang weightlessly through the Young Men's Christian Association Satellite-3 Trampoline Room; his dance steps seemed more graceful after he had spun with a hundred robots and ten dozen women; he took the accelerated Berlitz drug-course in French (eschewing the faster electrocerebral-stimulation series, because of a rumored transference that might slow his reflexes later that summer); and he felt that he was beginning to *sound* better—he had hired a gabcoach, and he bake-ovened Restoration plays into his pillow (and hopefully, into his head) whenever he slept (generally every third day now)—so that, as the day of the Fête drew near, he began feeling like a Renaissance courtier (a tired one).

As he stared at Civilized Moore inside his groomer, Primitive Moore wondered how long that feeling would last.

Two days before Versailles he cultivated a uniform tan and decided what he was going to say to Leota this time:

—I love you? (Hell, no!)

—Will you quit the cold circuit? (Uh-uh).

—If I join the Set, will you join me? (That seemed the best way to put it.)

Their third meeting, then, was to be on different terms. No more stakeouts in the wastes of the prosaic. The hunter was going to enter the brush. "Onward!" grinned the Moore in the groomer, "and Excelsior!"

She was dressed in a pale blue, mutie orchid corsage. The revolving dome of the palace spun singing zodiacs and the floors fluoresced witch-fires. He had the uncomfortable feeling that the damned flowers were growing there, right above her left breast, like an exotic parasite; and he resented their intrusion with a parochial possessiveness that he knew was not of the Renaissance. Nevertheless . . .

"Good evening. How do your flowers grow?"

"Barely, and quite contrary," she decided, sipping something green through a long straw, "but they cling to life."

"With an understandable passion," he noted, taking her hand which she did not withdraw. "Tell me, Eve of the Microprosopos—where are you headed?"

Interest flickered across her face and came to rest in her eyes.

"Your French has improved, Adam—Kadmon . . . ?" she noted. "I'm headed ahead. Where are you headed?"

"The same way."

"I doubt it—unfortunately."

"Doubt all you want, but we're parallel flows already."

"Is that a conceit drawn from some engineering laureate?"

"Watch me engineer a cold-bunk," he stated.

Her eyes shot X-rays through him, warming his bones.

"I knew you had something on your mind. If you were serious . . ."

"Us fallen spirits have to stick together here in Malkuth—I'm serious." He coughed and talked eyetalk. "Shall we stand together as though we're dancing? I see Unger; he sees us, and I want you."

"All right."

She placed her glass on a drifting tray and followed him out onto the floor and beneath the turning zodiac, leaving Setman Unger to face a labyrinth of flesh. Moore laughed at his predicament.

"It's harder to tell identities at an anti-costume party."

She smiled.

"You know, you dance differently today than last night."

"I know. Listen, how do I get a private iceberg and a key to Schlerafenland? I've decided it might be amusing. I know that it's not a matter of genealogy, or even money, for that matter, although both seem to help. I've read all the literature, but I could use some practical advice."

Her hand quivered ever so slightly in his own.

"You know the Doyenne?" she said/asked.

"Mainly rumors," he replied, "to the effect that she's an old gargoyle they've frozen to frighten away the Beast come Armageddon."

Leota did not smile. Instead, she became an arrow again.

"More or less," she replied coldly. "She does keep beastly people out of the Set."

Civilized Moore bit his tongue.

"Although many do not like her," she continued, becoming slightly more animated as she reflected, "I've always found her a rare little piece of chinoiserie. I'd like to take her home, if I had a home, and set her on my mantel, if I had a mantel."

"I've heard that she'd fit right into the Victorian Room at the NAM Galleries," Moore ventured.

"She *was* born during Vicky's reign—and she *was* in her eighties when the cold-bunk was developed—but I can safely say that the matter goes no further."

"And she decided to go gallivanting through Time at that age?"

"Precisely," answered Leota, "inasmuch as she wishes to be the immortal arbiter of trans-society."

They turned with the music. Leota had relaxed once more.

"At one hundred and ten she's already on her way to becoming an archetype," Moore noted. "Is that one of the reasons interviews are so hard to come by?"

"One of the reasons. . . ." she told him. "If, for example, you were to petition Party Set now, you would still have to wait until next summer for the interview—provided you reached that stage."

"How many are there on the roster of eligibles?"

She shut her eyes.

"I don't know. Thousands, I should say. She'll only see a few dozen, of course. The others will have been weeded out, pruned off, investigated away, and variously disqualified by the directors. Then, naturally, *she* will have the final say as to who is *in*."

Suddenly green and limpid—as the music, the lights, the ultrasonics, and the delicate narcotic fragrances of the air altered subtly—the room became a dark, cool place at the bottom of the sea, heady and nostalgic as the mind of a mermaid staring upon the ruins of Atlantis. The elegiac genius of the hall drew them closer together by a kind of subtle gravitation, and she was cool and adhesive as he continued:

"What is her power, really? I've read the tapes; I know she's a big stockholder, but so what? Why can't the directors vote around her? If I paid out—"

"They *wouldn't*," she said. "Her money means nothing. She is an institution.

"Hers is the quality of exclusiveness which keeps the Set the Set," she went on. "Imitators will always fail because they lack her discrimination. They'll take in any boorish body who'll pay. *That* is the reason that People Who Count," (she pronounced the capitals), "will neither attend nor sponsor any but Set functions. All exclusiveness would vanish from the Earth if the Set lowered its standards."

"Money is money," said Moore. "If others paid the same for their parties . . ."

". . . Then the People who take their money would cease to Count. The Set would boycott them. They would lose their élan, be looked upon as hucksters."

"It sounds like a rather vicious moebius."

"It is a caste system with checks and balances. Nobody really wants it to break down."

"Even those who wash out?"

"Silly! They'd be the last. There's nothing to stop them from buying their own bunkers, if they can afford it, and waiting another five years to try again. They'd be wealthier anyhow for the wait, if they invest properly. Some have waited decades, and are still waiting. Some have made it after years of persisting. It makes the game more interesting, the achievement more satisfying. In a world of physical ease, brutal social equality, and reasonable economic equality, exclusiveness in frivolity becomes the most sought-after of all distinctions."

" 'Commodities,' " he corrected.

"No," she stated, "it is not for sale. Try buying it if money is all you have to offer."

That brought his mind back to more immediate considerations.

"What *is* the cost, if all the other qualifications are met?"

"The rule on that is sufficiently malleable to permit an otherwise qualified person to meet his dues. He guarantees his tenure, bunk-wise or Party-wise, until such a time as his income offsets his debt. So if he only possesses a modest fortune, he may still be quite eligible. This is necessary if we are to preserve our democratic ideals."

She looked away, looked back.

"Usually a step-scale of percentages on the returns from his investments is arranged. In fact, a Set counselor will be right there when you liquidate your assets, and he'll recommend the best conversions."

"Set must clean up on this."

"*Certainement*. It *is* a business, and the Parties don't come cheaply. But then, you'd be a part of Set yourself—being a shareholder is one of the membership requirements—and we're a restricted corporation, paying high dividends. Your principal will grow. If you were to be accepted, join, and then quit after even one objective month, something like twenty actual years would have passed. You'd be a month older and much wealthier when you leave—and perhaps somewhat wiser."

"Where do I go to put my name on the list?"

He knew, but he had hopes.

"We can call it in tonight, from here. There is always someone in the office. You will be visited in a week or so, after the preliminary investigation."

"Investigation?"

"Nothing to worry about. Or have you a criminal record, a history of insanity, or a bad credit rating?"

Moore shook his head.

"No, no, and no."

"Then you'll pass."

"But will I actually have a chance of getting in, against all those others?"

It was as though a single drop of rain fell upon his chest.

"Yes," she replied, putting her cheek into the hollow of his neck and staring out over his shoulder so that he could not see her expression, "you'll make it all the way to the lair of Mary Maude Mullen with a member sponsoring you. That final hurdle will depend on yourself."

"Then I'll make it," he told her.

". . . The interview may only last seconds. She's quick; her decisions are almost instantaneous, and she's never wrong."

"Then I'll make it," he repeated, exulting.
Above them, the zodiac rippled.

Moore found Darryl Wilson in a barmat in the Poconos. The actor had gone to seed; he was not the man Moore remembered from the award-winning frontier threelie series. That man had been a crag-browed, bushy-faced Viking of the prairies. In four years' time a facial avalanche had occurred, leaving its gaps and runnels across his expensive frown and dusting the face fur a shade lighter. Wilson had left it that way and cauterized his craw with the fire water he had denied the Red Man weekly. Rumor had it he was well into his second liver.

Moore sat beside him and inserted his card into the counter slot. He punched out a Martini and waited. When he noticed that the man was unaware of his presence, he observed, "You're Darryl Wilson and I'm Alvin Moore. I want to ask you something."

The straight-shooting eyes did not focus.

"News media man?"

"No, an old fan of yours," he lied.

"Ask away then," said the still-familiar voice. "You are a camera."

"Mary Maude Mullen, the bitch-goddess of the Set," he said. "What's she like?"

The eyes finally focused.

"You up for deification this session?"

"That's right."

"What do you think?"

Moore waited, but there were no more words, so he finally asked, "About what?"

"Anything. You name it."

Moore took a drink. He decided to play the game if it would make the man more tractable.

"I think I like Martinis," he stated. "Now—"

"Why?"

Moore growled. Perhaps Wilson was too far gone to be of any help. Still, one more try . . .

"Because they're relaxing and bracing, both at the same time, which is something I need after coming all this way."

"Why do you want to be relaxed and braced?"

"Because I prefer it to being tense and unbraced."

"Why?"

"What the hell is all this?"

"You lose. Go home."

Moore stood.

"Suppose I go out again and come back in and we start over? Okay?"

"Sit down. My wheels turn slowly but they still turn," said Wilson. "We're talking about the same thing. You want to know what Mary Maude is like? That's what she's like—all interrogatives. Useless ones. Attitudes are a disease that no one's immune to, and they vary so easily in the same person. In two minutes she'll have you stripped down to them, and your answers will depend on biochemistry and the weather. So will her decision. There's nothing I can tell you. She's pure caprice. She's life. She's ugly."

"That's all?"

"She refuses the wrong people. That's enough. Go away."

Moore finished his Martini and went away.

That winter Moore made a fortune. A modest one, to be sure.

He quit his job for a position with the Akwa Mining Research Lab, Oahu Division. It added ten minutes to his commuting time, but the title, Processing Director, sounded better than Assistant Division Chief, and he was anxious for a new sound. He did not slacken the pace of his force-fed social acceptability program, and one of its results was a January lawsuit.

The Set, he had been advised, preferred divorced male candidates to the perpetually single sort. For this reason, he had consulted a highly-rated firm of marriage contractors and entered into a three-month renewable, single partner drop-option contract, with Diane Demetrios, an unemployed model of Greek-Lebanese extraction.

One of the problems of modeling, he decided later, was that there were too many surgically-perfected female eidolons in the labor force; it was a rough profession in which to stay employed. His newly-acquired status had been sufficient inducement to cause Diane to press a breach of promise suit on the basis of an alleged oral agreement that the option *would* be renewed.

Burgess Social Contracting Services of course sent a properly obsequious adjuster, and they paid the court costs as well as the medfees for Moore's broken nose. (Diane had hit him with *The Essentials of Dress Display,* a heavy, illustrated talisman of a manual, which she carried about in a plastic case—as he slept beside their pool—plastic case and all.)

So, by the month of March, Moore felt ready and wise and capable of facing down the last remaining citizen of the nineteenth century.

By May, though, he was beginning to feel he had overtrained. He was tempted to take a month's psychiatric leave from his work, but he recalled Leota's question about a history of insanity. He vetoed the notion and thought of Leota. The world stood still as his mind turned. Guiltily, he realized that he had not thought of her for months. He had been too busy with his autodidactics, his new job, and Diane Demetrios to think of the Setqueen, his love.

He chuckled.

Vanity, he decided; I want her because everyone wants her.

No, that wasn't true either, exactly. . . . He wanted —what?

He thought upon his motives, his desires.

He realized, then, that his goals had shifted; the

act had become the actor. What he really wanted, first and foremost, impure and unsimple, was an in to the Set—that century-spanning stratocruiser, luxury class, jetting across tomorrow and tomorrow and all the days that followed after—to ride high, like those gods of old who appeared at the rites of the equinoxes, slept between precessions, and were re-manifest with each new season, the bulk of humanity living through all those dreary days that lay between. To be a part of Leota was to be a part of the Set, and that was what he wanted now. So of course it was vanity. It was love.

He laughed aloud. His autosurf initialed the blue lens of the Pacific like a manned diamond, casting the sharp cold chips of its surface up and into his face.

Returning from absolute zero, Lazarus-like, is neither painful nor disconcerting, at first. There are no sensations at all until one achieves the temperature of a reasonably warm corpse. By that time though, an injection of nirvana flows within the body's thawed rivers.

It is only when consciousness begins to return, thought Mrs. Mullen, to return with sufficient strength so that one fully realizes what has occurred—that the wine has survived another season in an uncertain cellar, its vintage grown rarer still—only then does an unpronounceable fear enter into the mundane outlines of the bedroom furniture—for a moment.

It is more a superstitious attitude than anything, a mental quaking at the possibility that the stuff of life, one's own life, has in some indefinable way been tampered with. A microsecond passes, and then only the dim recollection of a bad dream remains.

She shivered, as though the cold was still locked within her bones, and she shook off the notion of nightmares past.

She turned her attention to the man in the white coat who stood at her elbow.

"What day is it?" she asked him.

He was a handful of dust in the winds of Time. . . . .

"August eighteen, two thousand-two," answered the handful of dust. "How do you feel?"

"Excellent, thank you," she decided. "I've just touched upon a new century—this makes three I've visited—so why shouldn't I feel excellent? I intend to visit many more."

"I'm sure you will, madam."

The small maps of her hands adjusted the counterpane. She raised her head.

"Tell me what is new in the world."

The doctor looked away from the sudden acetylene burst behind her eyes.

"We have finally visited Neptune and Pluto," he narrated. "They are quite uninhabitable. It appears that man is alone in the solar system. The Lake Sahara project has run into more difficulties, but it seems that work may begin next spring now that those stupid French claims are near settlement. . . ."

Her eyes fused his dust to planes of glass.

"Another competitor, Futuretime Gay, entered into the time-tank business three years ago," he recited, trying to smile, "but we met the enemy and they are ours—Set bought them out eight months ago. By the way, our own bunkers are now much more sophistica—"

"I repeat," she said, "what is new in the world, *Doctor?*"

He shook his head, avoiding the look she gave him.

"We can lengthen the remissions now," he finally told her, "quite a time beyond what could be achieved by the older methods."

"A better delaying action?"

"Yes."

"But not a cure?"

He shook his head.

"In my case," she told him, "it has already been

abnormally delayed. The old nostrums have already worn thin. For how long are the new ones good?"

"We still don't know. You have an unusual variety of M.S. and it's complicated by other things."

"Does a cure seem any nearer?"

"It could take another twenty years. We might have one tomorrow."

"I see." The brightness subsided. "You may leave now, young man. Turn on my advice tape as you go."

He was glad to let the machine take over.

Diane Demetrios dialed the library and requested the Setbook. She twirled the page-dial and stopped.

She studied the screen as though it were a mirror, her face undergoing a variety of expressions.

"I look just as good," she decided after a time. "Better, even. Your nose could be changed, and your browline . . .

"If they weren't facial fundamentalists," she told the picture, "if they didn't discriminate against surgery, lady—you'd be here and I'd be there.

"Bitch!"

The millionth barrel of converted seawater emerged, fresh and icy, from the Moore Purifier. Splashing from its chamber-tandem and flowing through the conduits, it was clean, useful, and singularly unaware of these virtues. Another transfusion of briny Pacific entered at the other hand.

The waste products were used in pseudoceramicware.

The man who designed the double-duty Purifier was rich.

The temperature was 82° in Oahu.

The million-first barrel splashed forth. . . .

They left Alvin Moore surrounded by china dogs.

Two of the walls were shelved, floor to ceiling. The shelves were lined with blue, green, pink, russet (not to mention ochre, vermilion, mauve, and saffron) dogs, mainly glazed (although some were dry-rubbed primitives), ranging from the size of a largish cockroach up to that of a pigmy warthog. Across the room a veritable Hades of a wood fire roared its metaphysical challenge into the hot July of Bermuda.

Set above it was a mantelpiece bearing more dogs.

Set beside the hellplace was a desk, at which was seated Mary Maude Mullen, wrapped in a green and black tartan. She studied Moore's file, which lay open on the blotter. When she spoke to him she did not look up.

Moore stood beside the chair which had not been offered him and pretended to study the dogs and the heaps of Georgian kindling that filled the room to overflowing.

While not overly fond of live dogs, Moore bore them no malice. But when he closed his eyes for a moment he experienced a feeling of claustrophobia.

These were not dogs. These were the unblinking aliens staring through the bars of the last Earthman's cage. Moore promised himself that he would say nothing complimentary about the garish rainbow of a hound pack (fit, perhaps, for stalking a jade stag the size of a Chihuahua); he decided it could only have sprung from the mental crook of a monomaniac, or one possessed of a very feeble imagination and small respect for dogs.

After verifying all the generalities listed on his petition, Mrs. Mullen raised her pale eyes to his.

"How do you like my doggies?" she asked him.

She sat there, a narrow-faced, wrinkled woman with flaming hair, a snub nose, an innocent expression, and the lingering twist of the question quirking her thin lips.

Moore quickly played back his last thoughts and decided to maintain his integrity in regards china dogs by answering objectively.

"They're quite colorful," he noted.

This was the wrong answer, he felt, as soon as he said it. The question had been too abrupt. He had entered the study ready to lie about anything but china dogs. So he smiled.

"There are a dreadful lot of them about. But of course they don't bark or bite or shed, or do other things. . . ."

She smiled back.

"My dear little, colorful bitches and sons of bitches," she said. "They don't do anything. They're sort of symbolic. That's why I collect them, too.

"Sit down"—she gestured—"and pretend you're comfortable."

"Thanks."

"It says here that you rose only recently from the happy ranks of anonymity to achieve some sort of esoteric distinction in the sciences. Why do you wish to resign it now?"

"I wanted money and prestige, both of which I was given to understand would be helpful to a Set candidate."

"Aha! Then they were a means rather than an end?"

"That is correct."

"Then tell me why you want to join the Set."

He had written out the answer to that one months ago. It had been bake-ovened into his brain, so that he could speak it with natural inflections. The words began forming themselves in his throat, but he let them die there. He had planned them for what he had thought would be maximum appeal to a fan of Tennyson's. Now he was not so sure.

Still . . . He broke down the argument and picked a neutral point—the part about following knowledge like a sinking star.

"There will be a lot of changes over the next several decades. I'd like to see them with a young man's eyes."

"As a member of the Set you will exist more to be seen than to see," she replied, making a note in his file. ". . . And I think we'll have to dye your hair if we accept you."

"The hell you say!—Pardon me, that slipped out."

"Good." She made another note. "We can't have them too inhibited—nor too uninhibited, for that matter. Your reaction was rather quaint." She looked up again.

"Why do you want so badly to see the future?"

He felt uneasy. It seemed as though she knew he was lying.

"Plain human curiosity," he answered weakly, "as well as some professional interest. Being an engineer—"

"We're not running a seminar," she observed. "You'd not be wasting much time outside of attending Parties if you wanted to last very long with the Set. In twenty years—no, ten—you'll be back in kindergarten so far as engineering is concerned. It will all be hieroglyphics to you. You don't read hieroglyphics, do you?"

He shook his head.

"Good," she continued. "I have an inept comparison. Yes, it will all be hieroglyphics, and if you should leave the Set you would be an unskilled draftsman—not that you'd have need to work. But if you were to want to work, you would have to be self-employed—which grows more and more difficult, almost too difficult to attempt, as time moves on. You should doubtless lose money."

He shrugged and raised his palms. He *had* been thinking of doing that. Fifty years, he had told himself, and we could kick the Set, be rich, and I could take refresher courses and try for a consultantship in marine engineering.

"I'd know enough to appreciate things, even if I couldn't participate," he explained.

"You'd be satisfied just to observe?"

"I think so," he lied.

"I doubt it." Her eyes nailed him again. "Do you think you are in love with Leota Mason? She nominated you, but of course that *is* her privilege."

"I don't know," he finally said. "I thought so at first, two years ago. . . ."

"Infatuation is fine," she told him. "It makes for good gossip. Love, on the other hand, I will not tolerate. Purge yourself of such notions. Nothing is so boring and ungay at a Set affair. It does not make for gossip; it makes for snickers.

"So is it infatuation or love?"

"Infatuation," he decided.

She glanced into the fire, glanced at her hands.

"You will have to develop a Buddhist's attitude toward the world around you. That world will change from day to day. Whenever you stop to look at it, it will be a different world—unreal."

He nodded.

"Therefore, if you are to maintain your stability, the Set must be the center of all things. Wherever your heart lies, there also shall reside your soul."

He nodded again.

". . . And if you should happen not to like the future, whenever you do stop to take a look at it, remember, you *cannot* come back. Don't just think about that, *feel* it!"

He felt it.

She began jotting. Her right hand began suddenly to tremble. She dropped the pen and too carefully drew her hand back within the shawl.

"You are not so colorful as most candidates," she told him, too naturally, "but then, we're short on the soulful type at present. Contrast adds depth and texture to our displays. Go view all the tapes of our past Parties."

"I already have."

". . . And you can give your soul to that, or a significant part thereof?"

"Wherever my heart lies . . ."

"In that case, you may return to your lodgings, Mister Moore. You will receive our decision today."

Moore stood. There were so many questions he had not been asked, so many things he had wanted to say, had forgotten, or had not had opportunity to say. . . . Had she already decided to reject him? he wondered. Was that why the interview had been so brief? Still, her final remarks *had* been encouraging.

He escaped from the fragile kennel, all his pores feeling like fresh nail holes.

He lolled about the hotel pool all afternoon, and in the evening he moved into the bar. He did not eat dinner.

When he received the news that he had been accepted, he was also informed by the messenger that a small gift to his inquisitor was a thing of custom. Moore laughed drunkenly, foreseeing the nature of the gift.

Mary Maude Mullen received her first Pacificware dog from Oahu with a small, sad shrug that almost turned to a shudder. She began to tremble then, nearly dropping it from her fingers. Quickly, she placed it on the bottommost shelf behind her desk and reached for her pills; later, the flames caused it to crack.

They were dancing. The sea was an evergreen-gold sky above the dome. The day was strangely young.

Tired remnants of the Party's sixteen hours, they clung to one another, feet aching, shoulders sloped. There were eight couples still moving on the floor, and the weary musicians fed them the slowest music they could make. Sprawled at the edges of the world, where the green bowl of the sky joined with the blue tiles of the Earth, some five hundred people, garments loosened, mouths open, stared like goldfish on a tabletop at the water behind the wall.

"Think it'll rain?" he asked her.

"Yes," she answered.

"So do I. So much for the weather. Now, about that week on the moon—?"

"What's wrong with good old Mother Earth?" she smiled.

Someone screamed. The sound of a slap occurred almost simultaneously. The screaming stopped.

"I've never been to the moon," he replied.

She seemed faintly amused.

"I have. I don't like it."

"Why?"

"It's the cold, crazy lights outside the dome," she said, "and the dark, dead rocks everywhere around the dome," she winced. "They make it seem like a cemetery at the end of Time. . . ."

"Okay," he said, "forget it."

". . . And the feeling of disembodied lightness as you move about inside the dome—"

"All right!"

"I'm sorry." She brushed his neck with her lips. He touched her forehead with his. "The Set has lost its shellac," she smiled.

"We're not on tape anymore. It doesn't matter now."

A woman began sobbing somewhere near the giant sea horse that had been the refreshment table. The musicians played more loudly. The sky was full of luminescent starfish, swimming moistly on their tractor beams. One of the starfish dripped salty water on them as it passed overhead.

"We'll leave tomorrow," he said.

"Yes, tomorrow," she said.

"How about Spain?" he said. "This is the season of the sherries. There'll be the Juegos Florales de la Vendimia Jerezana. It may be the last."

"Too noisy," she said, "with all those fireworks."

"But gay."

"Gay," she sighed with a crooked mouth. "Let's go to Switzerland and pretend we're old, or dying of something romantic."

"Necrophilist," he grinned, slipping on a patch of moisture and regaining his balance. "Better it be a quiet loch in the Highlands, where you can have your fog and miasma and I can have my milk and honeydew unblended."

"Nay," she said, above a quick babble of drunken voices, "let's go to New Hampshire."

"What's wrong with Scotland?"

"I've never been to New Hampshire."

"I have, and *I* don't like it. It looks like your description of the moon."

A moth brushing against a candle flame, the tremor.

The frozen bolt of black lightning lengthened slowly in the green heavens. A sprinkling of soft rain began.

As she kicked off her shoes he reached out for a glass on the floating tray above his left shoulder. He drained it and replaced it.

"Tastes like someone's watering the drinks."

"Set must be economizing," she said.

Moore saw Unger then, glass in hand, standing at the edge of the floor watching them.

"I see Unger."

"So do I. He's swaying."

"So are we," he laughed.

The fat bard's hair was a snowy chaos and his left eye was swollen nearly shut. He collapsed with a bubbling murmur, spilling his drink. No one moved to help him.

"I believe he's overindulged himself again."

"Alas, poor Unger," she said without expression, "I knew him well."

The rain continued to fall and the dancers moved about the floor like the figures in some amateur puppet show.

"They're coming!" cried a non-Setman, crimson cloak flapping. "They're coming down!"

The water streamed into their eyes as every conscious head in the Party Dome was turned upward. Three silver zeppelins grew in the cloudless green.

"They're coming for us," observed Moore.

"They're going to make it!"

The music had paused momentarily, like a pendulum at the end of its arc. It began again.

Good night, ladies, played the band, *good night, ladies* . . .

"We're going to live!"

"We'll go to Utah," he told her, eyes moist, "where they don't have seaquakes and tidal waves."

"Good night ladies . . ."

"We're going to live!"

She squeezed his hand.

"Merrily we roll along," the voices sang, *"roll along . . ."*

" 'Roll along,' " she said.

" 'Merrily,' " he answered.

"O'er the deep blue sea!"

A Set-month after the nearest thing to a Set disaster on record (that is to say, in the year of Our Lord and President Cambert 2019, twelve years after the quake), Setman Moore and Leota (nee Lachesis) stood outside the Hall of Sleep on Bermuda Island. It was almost morning.

"I believe I love you," he mentioned.

"Fortunately, love does not require an act of faith," she noted, accepting a light for her cigar, "because I don't believe in anything."

"Twenty years ago I saw a lovely woman at a Party and I danced with her."

"Five weeks ago," she amended.

"I wondered then if she would ever consider quitting the Set and going human again, and being heir to mortal ills."

"I have often wondered that myself," she said, "in idle moments. But she won't do it. Not until she is old and ugly."

"That means forever," he smiled sadly.

"You *are* noble." She blew smoke at the stars, touched the cold wall of the building. "Someday, when people no longer look at her, except for purposes of comparison with some fluffy child of the far future—or when the world's standards of beauty have changed—then she'll transfer from the express run to the local and let the rest of the world go by."

"Whatever the station, she will be all alone in a strange town," said Moore. "Every day, it seems, they remodel the world. I met a fraternity brother at that dinner last night—pardon me, last year—and he treated me as if he were my father. His every other word was 'son' or 'boy' or 'kid,' and he wasn't trying to be funny. He was responding to what he saw. My appetite was considerably diminished.

"Do you realize where we're going?" he asked the back of her head as she turned away to look out over the gardens of sleeping flowers. "Away! That's where. We can never go back! The world moves on while we sleep."

"Refreshing, isn't it?" she finally said. "And stimulating, and awe-inspiring. Not being bound, I mean. Everything burning. Us remaining. Neither time nor space can hold us, unless we consent.

"And I do not consent to being bound," she declared.

"To anything?"

"To anything."

"Supposing it's all a big joke."

"What?"

"The world. —Supposing every man, woman, and child died last year in an invasion by creatures from

Alpha Centauri, everyone but the frozen Set. Supposing it was a totally effective virus attack. . . ."

"There are no creatures in the Centauri System. I read that the other day."

"Okay, someplace else then. Supposing all the remains and all the traces of chaos were cleaned up, and then one creature gestured with a flipper at this building." Moore slapped the wall. "The creature said: 'Hey! There are some live ones inside, on ice. Ask one of the sociologists whether they're worth keeping, or if we should open the refrigerator door and let them spoil.' Then one of the sociologists came and looked at us, all in our coffins of ice, and *he* said: 'They might be worth a few laughs and a dozen pages in an obscure periodical. So let's fool them into thinking that everything is going on just as it was before the invasion. All their movements, according to these schedules, are pre-planned, so it shouldn't be too difficult. We'll fill their Parties with human simulacra packed with recording machinery and we'll itemize their behavior patterns. We'll vary their circumstances and they'll attribute it to progress. We can watch them perform in all sorts of situations that way. Then, when we're finished, we can always break their bunktimers and let them sleep on—or open their doors and watch them spoil.'

"So they agreed to do it," finished Moore, "and here we are, the last people alive on Earth, cavorting before machines operated by inhuman creatures who are watching us for incomprehensible reasons."

"Then we'll give them a good show," she replied, "and maybe they'll applaud us once before we spoil."

She snubbed out her cigar and kissed him good night. They returned to their refrigerators.

It was twelve weeks before Moore felt the need for a rest from the Party circuit. He was beginning to grow fearful. Leota had spent nonfunctional decades of her time vacationing with him, and she had recently been showing signs of sullenness, apparently regretting these expenditures on his behalf. So he decided to see something real, to take a stroll in the year 2078. After all, he was over a hundred years old.

The Queen Will Live Forever, said the faded clipping that hung in the main corridor of the Hall of Sleep. Beneath the bannerline was the old/recent story of the conquest of the final remaining problems of Multiple Sclerosis, and the medical ransom of one of its most notable victims. Moore had not seen the Doyenne since the day of his interview. He did not care whether he ever saw her again.

He donned a suit from his casualware style locker and strolled through the gardens and out to the airfield. There were no people about.

He did not really know where he wanted to go until he stood before a ticket booth and the speaker asked him, "Destination, please."

"Uh—Oahu. Akwa Labs, if they have a landing field of their own."

"Yes, they do. That will have to be a private charter though, for the final fifty-six miles—"

"Give me a private charter all the way, both ways."

"Insert your card, please."

He did.

After five seconds the card popped back into his waiting hand. He dropped it into his pocket.

"What time will I arrive?" he asked.

"Nine hundred thirty-two, if you leave on Dart Nine six minutes from now. Have you any luggage?"

"No."

"In that case, your Dart awaits you in area A-11."

Moore crossed the field to the VTO Dart numbered "Nine." It flew by tape. The flight pattern, since it was a specially chartered run, had been worked out back at the booth, within milliseconds of

Moore's naming his destination. It was then broadcast-transferred to a blank tape inside Dart Nine; an auto-alternation brain permitted the Dart to correct its course in the face of unforeseen contingencies and later recorrect itself, landing precisely where it was scheduled to come down.

Moore mounted the ramp and stopped to slip his card into the slot beside the hatchway. The hatch swung open and he collected his card and entered. He selected a seat beside a port and snapped its belt around his middle. At this, the hatchway swung itself shut.

After a few minutes the belt unfastened itself and vanished into the arms of his seat. The Dart was cruising smoothly now.

"Do you wish to have the lights dimmed? Or would you prefer to have them brighter?" asked a voice at his side.

"They're fine just the way they are," he told the invisible entity.

"Would you care for something to eat? Or something to drink?"

"I'll have a Martini."

There was a sliding sound, followed by a muted click. A tiny compartment opened in the wall beside him. His Martini rested within.

He removed it and sipped a sip.

Beyond the port and toward the rear of the Dart, a faint blue nimbus arose from the sideplates.

"Would you care for anything else?" *Pause.* "Shall I read you an article on the subject of your choice?" *Pause.* "Or fiction?" *Pause.* "Or poetry?" *Pause.* "Would you care to view the catalog?" *Pause.* "Or perhaps you would prefer music?"

"Poetry?" repeated Moore.

"Yes, I have many of—"

"I know a poet," he remembered. "Have you anything by Wayne Unger?"

There followed a brief mechanical meditation, then:
"Wayne Unger. Yes," answered the voice. "On call are his *Paradise Unwanted, Fungi of Steel,* and *Chisel in the Sky.*"

"Which is his most recent work?" asked Moore.

"*Chisel in the Sky.*"

"Read it to me."

The voice began by reading him all the publishing data and copyright information. To Moore's protests it answered that it was a matter of law and cited a precedent case. Moore asked for another Martini and waited.

Finally, " '*Our Wintered Way Through Evening, and Burning Bushes Along It,*' " said the voice.

"Huh?"

"That is the title of the first poem."

"Oh, read on."

" '*(Where only the evergreens whiten . . .)*

*Winterflaked ashes heighten
in towers of blizzard.
Silhouettes unseal an outline.
Darkness, like an absence of faces,
pours from the opened home;
it seeps through shattered pine
and flows the fractured maple.*

*Perhaps it is the essence senescent,
dreamculled from the sleepers,
that soaks upon this road
in weather-born excess.
Or perhaps the great Anti-Life
learns to paint with a vengeance,
to run an icicle down the gargoyle's eye.*

*For properly speaking, though
no one can confront himself in toto,*

*I see your falling sky, gone gods,
as in a smoke-filled dream
of ancient statues burning,
soundlessly, down to the ground.*

(. . . and never the everwhite's green.)' "

There was a ten-second pause, then: "The next poem is entitled—"

"Wait a minute," asked Moore. "That first one—? Are you programmed to explain anything about it?"

"I am sorry, I am not. That would require a more complicated unit."

"Repeat the copyright date of the book."

"Two-thousand-sixteen, in the North American Union—"

"And it's his most recent work?"

"Yes, he is a member of the Party Set and there is generally a lapse of several decades between his books."

"Continue reading."

The machine read on. Moore knew little concerning verse, but he was struck by the continual references to ice and cold, to snow and sleep.

"Stop," he told the machine. "Have you anything of his from before he joined the Set?"

"*Paradise Unwanted* was published in 1981, two years after he became a member. According to its Foreword, however, most of it was written prior to his joining."

"Read it."

Moore listened carefully. It contained little of ice, snow, or sleep. He shrugged at this minor discovery. His seat immediately adjusted and readjusted to the movement.

He barely knew Unger. He did not like his poetry. He did not like most poetry, though.

The reader began another.

" *'In the Dogged House,'* " it said.

" *'The heart is a graveyard of crigas,
hid far from the hunter's eye,
where love wears death like enamel
and dogs crawl in to die . . .'* "

Moore smiled as it read the other stanzas. Recognizing its source, he liked that one somewhat better.

"Stop reading," he told the machine.

He ordered a light meal and thought about Unger. He had spoken with him once. When was it?

Two-thousand-seventeen . . . ? Yes, at the Free Workers' Liberation Centennial in the Lenin Palace.

It was rivers of vodka. . . .

Fountains of juices, like inhuman arteries slashed, spurted their bright umbrellas of purple and lemon and green and orange. Jewels to ransom an Emir flashed near many hearts. Their host, Premier Korlov, seemed a happy frost giant in his display.

. . . In a dance pavilion of polaroid crystal, with the World outside blinking off and on, on and off— like an advertisement, Unger had commented, both elbows resting on the bar top and his foot on the indispensable rail.

His head had swiveled as Moore approached. He was a bleary-eyed albino owl. "Albion Moore, I believe," he had said, extending a hand. "Quo vadis dammit?"

"Grape juice and wadka," said Moore to the unnecessary human standing beside the mix-machine. The uniformed man pressed two buttons and passed the glass across two feet of frosty mahogany. Moore twitched it toward Unger in a small salute. "A happy Free Workers' Liberation Centennial to you."

"I'll drink to liberation." The poet leaned foward and poked his own combination of buttons. The man in the uniform sniffed audibly.

They drank a drink together.

"They accuse us"—Unger's gesture indicated the world at large—"of neither knowing nor caring anything about un-Set things, un-Set people."

"Well, it's true, isn't it?"

"Oh yes, but it might be expanded upon. We're the same way with our fellows. Be honest now, how many Setmen are you acquainted with?"

"Quite a few."

"I didn't ask how many names you knew."

"Well, I talk with them all the time. Our environment is suited to much movement and many words—and we have all the time in the world. How many friends do *you* have?" he asked.

"I just finished one," grunted the poet, leaning forward. "I'm going to mix me another."

Moore didn't feel like being depressed or joked with and he was not sure which category this fell into. He had been living inside a soap bubble since after the ill-starred Davy Jones Party, and he did not want anyone poking sharp things in his direction.

"So, you're your own man. If you're not happy in the Set, leave."

"You're not being a true *tovarisch*," said Unger, shaking a finger. "There was a time when a man could tell his troubles to bartenders and barfriends. You wouldn't remember, though—those days went out when the nickle-plated barmatics came in. Damn their exotic eyes and scientific mixing!"

Suddenly he punched out three drinks in rapid succession. He slopped them across the dark, shiny surface.

"Taste them! Sip each of them!" he enjoined Moore. "Can't tell them apart without a scorecard, can you?"

"They're dependable that way."

"Dependable? Hell yes! Depend on them to create neurotics. One time a man could buy a beer and bend an ear. All that went out when the dependable mix-machines came in. Now we join a talk-out club of manic change and most unnatural! Oh, had the Mermaid been such!" he complained in false notes of frenzy. "Or the Bloody Lion of Stepney! What jaded jakes the fellows of Marlowe had been!"

He sagged.

"Aye! Drinking's not what it used to be."

The international language of his belch caused the mix-machine attendant to avert his face, which betrayed a pained expression before he did so.

"So I'll repeat my question," stated Moore, making conversation. "Why do you stay where you're unhappy? You could go open a real bar of your own, if that's what you'd like. It would probably be a success, now that I think of it—people serving drinks and all that."

"Go to! Go to! I shan't say where!" He stared at nothing. "Maybe that's what I'll do someday, though," he reflected, "open a real bar. . . ."

Moore turned his back to him then, to watch Leota dancing with Korlov. He was happy.

"People join the Set for a variety of reasons," Unger was muttering, "but the main one is exhibitionism, with the titillating wraith of immortality lurking at the stage door, perhaps. Attracting attention to oneself gets harder and harder as time goes on. It's almost impossible in the sciences. In the nineteenth and twentieth centuries you could still name great names—now it's great research teams. The arts have been democratized out of existence—and where have all the audiences gone? I don't mean spectators either.

"So we have the Set," he continued. "Take our sleeping beauty there, dancing with Korlov—"

"Huh?"

"Pardon me, I didn't mean to awaken you abruptly. I was saying that if she wanted attention Miss Mason couldn't be a stripper today, so she had to join the

Set. It's even better than being a threelie star, and it requires less work—"

"Stripper?"

"A folk artist who undressed to music."

"Yes, I recall hearing of them."

"That's gone too, though," sighed Unger, "and while I cannot disapprove of the present customs of dress and undress, it still seems to me as if something bright and frail died in the elder world."

"She *is* bright, isn't she?"

"Decidedly so."

They had taken a short walk then, outside, in the cold night of Moscow. Moore did not really want to leave, but he had had enough to drink so that he was easy to persuade. Besides that, he did not want the stumbling babbler at his side to fall into an excavation or wander off lost, to miss his flight or turn up injured. So they shuffled up bright avenues and down dim streets until they came to the Square. They stopped before a large, dilapidated monument. The poet broke a small limb from a shrub and bent it into a wreath. He tossed it against a wall.

"Poor fellow," he muttered.

"Who?"

"The guy inside."

"Who's that?"

Unger cocked his head at him.

"You really don't know?"

"I admit there are gaps in my education, if that's what you mean. I continually strive to fill them, but I always was weak on history. I specialized at an early age."

Unger jerked his thumb at the monument.

"Noble Macbeth lies in state within," he said. "He was an ancient king who slew his predecessor, noble Duncan, most heinously. Lost of other people too. When he took the throne he promised he'd be nice to his subjects, though. But the Slavic temperament is a strange thing. He is best remembered for his many fine speeches, which were translated by a man named Pasternak. Nobody reads them anymore."

Unger sighed and seated himself on a stair. Moore joined him. He was too cold to be insulted by the arrogant mocking of the drunken poet.

"Back then, people used to fight wars," said Unger.

"I know," responded Moore, his fingers freezing; "Napoleon once burnt part of this city."

Unger tipped his hat.

Moore scanned the skyline. A bewildering range of structures hedged the Square—here, bright and functional, a ladderlike office building composed its heights and witnessed distances, as only the planned vantages of the very new can manage; there, a daytime aquarium of an agency was now a dark mirror, a place where the confidence-inspiring efficiencies of rehearsed officials were displayed before the onlooker; and across the Square, its purged youth fully restored by shadow, a deserted onion of a cupola poked its sharp topknot after soaring vehicles, a number of which, scuttling among the star fires, were indicated even now—and Moore blew upon his fingers and jammed his hands into his pockets.

"Yes, nations went to war," Unger was saying. "Artilleries thundered. Blood was spilled. People died. But we lived through it, crossing a shaky Shinvat word by word. Then one day there it was. Peace. It had been that way a long time before anyone noticed. We still don't know how we did it. Perpetual postponement and a short memory, I guess, as man's attention became occupied twenty-four hours a day with other things. Now there is nothing left to fight over, and everyone is showing off the fruits of peace—because everyone has some, by the roomful. All they want. More. These things that fill the rooms, though," he mused, "and the mind—how they have proliferated! Each month's version is better than the last, in some hypersophisticated manner. They seem to have absorbed the minds that are absorbed with them. . . ."

"We could all go live in the woods," said Moore, wishing he had taken the time to pocket a battery crystal and a thermostat for his suit.

"We could do lots of things, and we will, eventually —I suppose. Still, I guess we *could* wind up in the woods, at that."

"In that case, let's go back to the Palace while there's still time. I'm frozen."

"Why not?"

They climbed to their feet, began walking back.

"Why *did* you join the Set anyhow? So you could be discontent over the centuries?"

"Nay, son," the poet clapped him on the shoulder. "I'm an audience in search of an entertainment."

It took Moore an hour to get the chill out of his bones.

"Ahem. Ahem," said the voice. "We are about to land at Akwa Labs, Oahu."

The belt snaked out into Moore's lap. He snapped it tight.

A sudden feeling prompted him to ask: "Read me that last poem from *Chisel* again."

" '*Future Be Not Impatient*,' " stated the voice:

" '*Someday, perhaps, but not this day.
Sometime; but then, not now.
Man is a monument-making mammal.
Never ask me how.*' "

He thought of Leota's description of the moon and he hated Unger for the forty-four seconds it took him to disembark. He was not certain why.

He stood beside Dart Nine and watched the approach of a small man wearing a smile and gay tropical clothing. He shook hands automatically.

". . . Very pleased," the man named Teng was saying, "and glad there's not much around for you to recognize anymore. We've been deciding what to show you ever since Bermuda called." Moore pretended to be aware of the call. ". . . Not many people remember their employers from as far back as you do," Teng was saying.

Moore smiled and fell into step with him, heading toward the Processing Complex.

"Yes, I was curious," he agreed, "to see what it all looks like now. My old office, my lab—"

"Gone, of course."

". . . our first chamber-tandem, with its big-nozzled injectors—"

"Replaced, naturally."

"Naturally. And the big old pumps . . ."

"Shiny and new."

Moore brightened. The sun, which he had not seen for several days/years, felt good on his back, but the air conditioning felt even better as they entered the first building. There was something of beauty in the pure functional compactness of everything about them, something Unger might have called by a different name, he realized, but it was beauty to Moore. He ran his hand along the sides of the units he did not have time to study. He tapped the conduits and peered into the kilns which processed the by-product ceramicware; he nodded approval and paused to relight his pipe whenever the man at his side asked his opinion of something too technically remote for him to have any opinion.

They crossed catwalks, moved through the temple-like innards of shut-down tanks, traversed alleyways where the silent, blinking panels indicated that unseen operations were in progress. Occasionally they met a worker, seated before a sleeping trouble-board, watching a broadcast entertainment or reading something over his portable threelie. Moore shook hands and forgot names.

Processing Director Teng could not help but be partly hypnotized—both by Moore's youthful appearance and the knowledge that he had developed a key process at some past date (as well as by his apparent understanding of present operations)—into believing that he was an engineer of his own breed, and up-to-date in his education. Actually, Mary Mullen's prediction that his profession would some day move beyond the range of his comprehension had not yet come to pass—but he could see that it was the direction in which he was headed. Appropriately, he had noticed his photo gathering dust in a small lobby, amid those of Teng's other dead and retired predecessors.

Sensing this feeling, Moore asked, "Say, do you think I could have my old job back?"

The man's head jerked about. Moore remained expressionless.

"Well—I suppose—something—could be worked . . ." he ended lamely as Moore broke into a grin and twisted the question back into casual conversation. It was somehow amusing to have produced that sudden, strange look of realization on the man's bored face, as he actually *saw* Moore for the first time. Frightening, too.

"Yes, seeing all this progress—is inspiring," Moore pronounced. "It's almost enough to make a man want to work again. Glad I don't have to, of course. But there's a bit of nostalgia involved in coming back after all these years and seeing how this place grew out of the shoestring operation it seemed then—grew into more buildings than I could walk through in a week, and all of them packed with new hardware and working away to beat the band. Smooth. Efficient. I like it. I suppose you like working here?"

"Yes," sighed Teng, "as much as a man can like

working. Say, were you planning on staying overnight? There a weekly employees' luau and you'd be very welcome." He glanced at the wafer of a watchface clinging to his wrist. "In fact, it's already started," he added.

"Thanks," said Moore, "but I have a date and I have to be going. I just wanted to reaffirm my faith in progress. Thanks for the tour, and thanks for your time."

"Any time," Teng steered him toward a lush Break Room. "You won't be wanting to Dart back for awhile yet, will you?" he said. "So while we're having a bite to eat in here I wonder if I could ask you some questions about the Set. Its entrance requirements in particular. . . ."

All the way around the world to Bermuda, getting happily drunk in the belly of Dart Nine, in the year of Our Lord 2078, Moore felt that Time had been put aright.

"So you want to have it?" said/asked Mary Maude, uncoiling carefully from the caverns of her shawl.

"Yes."

"Why?" she asked.

"Because I do not destroy that which belongs to me. I possess so very little as it is."

The Doyenne snorted gently, perhaps in amusement. She tapped her favorite dog, as though seeking a reply from it.

"Though it sails upon a bottomless sea toward some fabulous Orient," she mused, "the ship will still attempt to lower an anchor. I do not know why. Can you tell me? Is it simply carelessness on the part of the captain? Or the second mate?"

The dog did not answer. Neither did anything else.

"Or is it a mutineer's desire to turn around and go back?" she inquired. "To return home?"

There was a brief stillness. Finally:

"I live in a succession of homes. They are called hours. Each is lovely."

"But not lovely enough, and never to be revisited, eh? Permit me to anticipate your next words: 'I do not intend to marry. I do not intend to leave the Set. I shall have my child—' By the way, what will it be, a boy or a girl?"

"A girl."

" '—I shall have my daughter. I shall place her in a fine home, arrange her a glorious future, and be back in time for the Spring Festival.' " She rubbed her glazed dog as though it were a crystal and pretended to peer through its greenish opacity. "Am I not a veritable gypsy?" she asked.

"Indeed."

"And you think this will work out?"

"I fail to see why it should not."

"Tell me which her proud father will do," she inquired, "compose her a sonnet sequence, or design her mechanical toys?"

"Neither. He shall never know. He'll be asleep until spring, and I will not. *She* must never know either."

"So much the worse."

"Why, pray tell?"

"Because she will become a woman in less than two months, by the clocks of the Set—and a lovely woman, I daresay—because she will be able to afford loveliness."

"Of course."

"And, as the daughter of a member, she will be eminently eligible for Set candidacy."

"She may not want it."

"Only those who cannot achieve it allude to having those sentiments. No, she'll want it. Everyone does. And, if her beauty should be surgically obtained, I believe that I shall, in this instance, alter a rule of mine. I shall pass on her and admit her to the Set. She will then meet many interesting people—poets, engineers, her mother...."

"No! I'd tell her, before I'd permit that to happen!"

"Aha! Tell me, is your fear of incest predicated upon your fear of competition, or is it really the other way around?"

"Please! Why are you saying these horrible things?"

"Because, unfortunately, you are something I can no longer afford to keep around. You have been an excellent symbol for a long time, but now your pleasures have ceased to be Olympian. Yours is a lapse into the mundane. You show that the gods are less sophisticated than schoolchildren—that they can be victimized by biology, despite the oceans of medical allies at our command. Princess, in the eyes of the world you are my daughter, for I am the Set. So take some motherly advice and retire. Do not attempt to renew your option. Get married first, and then to sleep for a few months—till spring, when your option is up. Sleep intermittently in the bunker, so that a year or so will pass. We'll play up the romantic aspects of your retirement. Wait a year or two to bear your child. The cold sleep won't do her any harm; there have been other cases such as yours. If you fail to agree to this, our motherly admonition is that you will face present expulsion."

"You *can't!*"

"Read your contract."

"But no one need ever know!"

"You silly little dollface!" The acetylene blazed forth. "Your glimpses of the outside world have been fragmentary and extremely selective—for at least sixty years. Every news medium in the world watches almost every move every Setman makes, from the time he sits up in his bunker until he retires, exhausted, after the latest Party. Snoopers and newshounds today have more gimmicks and gadgets in their arsenals than your head has colorful hairs. We *can't* hide your daughter all her life, so we won't even try. We'd have enough trouble concealing matters if you decided not to have her—but I think we could outbribe and outdrug our own employees.

"Therefore, I call upon you for a decision."

"I am sorry."

"So am I," said the Doyenne.

The girl stood.

From somewhere, as she left, she seemed to hear the whimpering of a china dog.

Beyond the neat hedgerows of the garden and down a purposefully irregular slope ran the unpaved pathway which wandered, like an impulsive river, through neck-tickling straits of unkempt forsythia, past high islands of mobbed sumac, and by the shivering branches, like waves, of an occasional ginkgo, wagging at the overhead gulls, while dreaming of the high-flying Archaeopteryx about to break through its heart in a dive; and perhaps a thousand feet of twistings are required to negotiate the two hundred feet of planned wilderness that separates the gardens of the Hall of Sleep from the artificial ruins which occupy a full, hilly acre, dotted here and there by incipient jungles of lilac and the occasional bell of a great willow—which momentarily conceal, and then guide the eye on toward broken pediments, smashed friezes, half-standing, shred-topped columns, then fallen columns, then faceless, handless statues, and finally, seemingly random heaps of rubble which lay amid these things; here, the path over which they moved then forms a delta and promptly loses itself where the tides of Time chafe away the memento mori quality that the ruins first seem to spell, acting as a temporal entasis and in the eye of the beholding Setman, so that he can look upon it all and say, "I am older than this," and his companion can reply,

"We will pass again some year and this too, will be gone," (even though she did not say it this time) feeling happier by feeling the less mortal by so doing; and crossing through the rubble, as they did, to a place where barbarously ruined Pan grins from inside the ring of a dry fountain, a new path is to be located, this time an unplanned and only recently formed way, where the grass is yellowed underfoot and the walkers must go single file because it leads them through a place of briars, until they reach the old breakwall over which they generally climb like commandos in order to gain access to a quarter mile strand of coved and deserted beach, where the sand is not quite so clean as the beaches of the town—which are generally sifted every third day—but where the shade is as intense, in its own way, as the sunlight, and there are flat rocks offshore for meditation.

"You're getting lazy," he commented, kicking off his shoes and digging his toes into the cool sand. "You didn't climb over."

"I'm getting lazy," she agreed.

They threw off their robes and walked to the water's edge.

"Don't push!"

"Come on. I'll race you to the rocks."

For once he won.

Loafing in the lap of the Atlantic, they could have been any two bathers in any place, in any time.

"I could stay here forever."

"It gets cold at nights, and if there's a bad storm you might catch something or get washed away."

"I meant," she amended, "if it could always be like this."

" '*Verweile doch, du bist so schön,*' " he reminded. "Faust lost a bet that way, remember? So would a Sleeper. Unger's got me reading again—Hey! What's the matter?"

"Nothing!"

"There's something wrong, little girl. Even I can tell."

"So what if there is?"

"So a lot, that's what. Tell me."

Her hand bridged the narrow channel between their rocks and found his. He rolled onto his side and stared at her satin-wet hair and her stuck-together eyelashes, the dimpled deserts of her cheeks, and the bloodied oasis of her mouth. She squeezed his hand.

"Let's stay here forever—despite the chill, and being washed away."

"You are indicating that—?"

"We could get off at this stop."

"I suppose. But—"

"But you like it now? You like the big charade?"

He looked away.

"I think you were right," she told him, "that night—many years ago."

"What night?"

"The night you said it was all a joke—that we are the last people alive on Earth, performing before machines operated by inhuman creatures who watch us for incomprehensible purposes. What are we but wave-patterns on an oscilloscope? I'm sick of being an object of contemplation!"

He continued to stare into the sea.

"I'm rather fond of the Set now," he finally responded. "At first I was ambivalent toward it. But a few weeks—years—ago I visited a place where I used to work. It was—different. Bigger. Better run. But more than that, actually. It wasn't just that it was filled with things I couldn't have guessed at fifty or sixty years ago. I had an odd feeling while I was there. I was with a little chatterbox of a Processing Director named Teng, and he was yammering away worse than Unger, and I was just staring at all those tandem-tanks and tiers of machinery that had grown up inside the shell of that first old building—sort of like inside a womb—and I suddenly felt that someday something was going to be born, born of steel and plastic and dancing electrons, in such a stainless, sunless place—and *that* something would be so fine that I would want to be there to see it. I couldn't dignify it by calling it a mystical experience or anything like that. It was just sort of a feeling I had. But if *that* moment could stay forever . . . Anyhow, the Set is my ticket to a performance I'd like to see."

"Darling," she began, "it is anticipation and recollection that fill the heart—never the sensation of the moment."

"Perhaps you are right. . . ."

His grip tightened on her hand as the tunnel between their eyes shortened. He leaned across the water and kissed the blood from her mouth.

"*Verweile doch . . .*"

"*. . . Du bist so schön.*"

It was the Party to end all Parties. The surprise announcement of Alvin Moore and Leota Mathilde Mason struck the Christmas Eve gathering of the Set as just the thing for the season. After an extensive dinner and the exchange of bright and costly trifles the lights were dimmed. The giant Christmas tree atop the transparent penthouse blazed like a compressed galaxy through the droplets of melted snow on the ceilingpane.

It was nine by all the clocks of London.

"Married on Christmas, divorced on Twelfth Night," said someone in the darkness.

"What'll they do for an encore?" whispered someone else.

There were giggles and several off-key carols followed them. The backlight pickup was doubtless in action.

"Tonight we are quaint," said Moore.

"We danced in Davy Jones' Locker," answered Leota, "while they cringed and were sick on the floor."

"It's not the same Set," he told her, "not really. How many new faces have you counted? How many old ones have vanished? It's hard to tell. Where do old Setmen go?"

"The graveyard of the elephants," she suggested. "Who knows?"

" *'The heart is a graveyard of crigas,'* " recited Moore,

" *'hid far from the hunter's eye,
where love wears death like enamel
and dogs crawl in to die.'* "

"That's Unger's, isn't it?" she asked.

"That's right, I just happened to recall it."

"I wish you hadn't. I don't like it."

"Sorry."

"Where is Unger anyway?" she asked as the darkness retreated and the people arose.

"Probably at the punch bowl—or under the table."

"Not this early in the evening—for being under the table, I mean."

Moore shifted.

"What *are* we doing here anyhow?" he wanted to know. "Why did we have to attend this Party?"

"Because it is the season of charity."

"Faith and hope, too," he smirked. "You want to be maudlin or something? All right, I'll be maudlin with you. It *is* a pleasure, really."

He raised her hand to his lips.

"Stop that!"

"All right."

He kissed her on the mouth. There was laughter.

She flushed but did not rise from his side.

"If you want to make a fool of me—of us," he said, "I'll go more than halfway. Tell me why we had to come to this Party and announce our un-Setness before everyone? We could have just faded away from the Parties, slept until spring, and let our options run out."

"No. I am a woman and I could not resist another Party—the last one of the year, the very last—and wear your gift on my finger and know that deep down inside, the others *do* envy us—our courage, if nothing else—and probably our happiness."

"Okay," he agreed, "I'll drink to it—to you, anyway." He raised his glass and downed it. There was no fireplace to throw it into, so as much as he admired the gesture he placed it back on the table.

"Shall we dance? I hear music."

"Not yet. Let's just sit here and drink."

"Fine."

When all the clocks in London said eleven, Leota wanted to know where Unger was.

"He left," a slim girl with purple hair told her, "right after dinner. Maybe indigestion"—she shrugged —"or maybe he went looking for the Globe."

She frowned and took another drink.

Then they danced. Moore did not really see the room through which they moved, nor the other dancers. They were all featureless characters in a book he had already closed. Only the dance was real—and the woman with whom he was dancing.

Time's friction, he decided, and a raising of the sights. I have what I wanted and still I want more. I'll get over it.

It was a vasty hall of mirrors. There were hundreds of Alvin Moores and Leotas (nee Mason) dancing. They were dancing at all their Parties of the past seventy-some years—from a Tibetan ski lodge to Davy Jones' Locker, from a New Year's Eve in orbit to the floating Palace of Kanayasha, from a Halloween in the caverns of Carlsbad to a May Day at

Delphi—they had danced everywhere, and tonight was the last Party, *good night, ladies*. . . .

She leaned against him and said nothing and her breath collared his neck.

"Good-night, good-night, good-night," he heard himself saying, and they left with the bells of midnight, early, early, and it was Christmas as they entered the hopcar and told the Set chauffeur that they were returning early.

And they passed over the stratocruiser and settled beside the Dart they had come in, and they crossed through the powdery fleece that lay on the ground and entered the smaller craft.

"Do you wish to have the lights dimmed? Or would you prefer to have them brighter?" asked a voice at their side, after London and its clocks and its Bridge had fallen, down.

"Dim them."

"Would you care for something to eat? Or something to drink?"

"No."

"No."

"Shall I read you an article on the subject of your choice?" *Pause.* "Or fiction?" *Pause.* "Or poetry?" *Pause.* "Would you care to view the catalog?" *Pause.* "Or perhaps you would prefer music?"

"Music," she said. "Soft. Not the kind you listen to."

After about ten minutes of near-sleep, Moore heard the voice:

"Hilted of flame,
our frail phylactic blade
slits black
beneath Polestar's
pinprick comment,
foredging burrs
of mitigated hell,
spilling light without illumination.

*Strands of song,
to share its stinging flight,
are shucked and scraped
to fit an idiot theme.
Here, through outlocked chaos,
climbed of migrant logic,
the forms of black notation
blackly dice a flame."*

"Turn it off," said Moore. "We didn't ask you to read."

"I'm not reading," said the voice. "I'm composing."

"Who—?"

Moore came awake and turned in his seat, which promptly adjusted to the movement. A pair of feet projected over the arm of a double seat to the rear.

"Unger?"

"No, Santa Claus. Ho! Ho!"

"What are you doing going back this early?"

"You just answered your own question, didn't you?"

Moore snorted and settled back once more. At his side, Leota was snoring delicately, her seat collapsed into a couch.

He shut his eyes, but knowing they were not alone he could not regain the peaceful drifting sensation he had formerly achieved. He heard a sigh and the approach of lurching footfalls. He kept his eyes closed, hoping Unger would fall over and go to sleep. He didn't.

Abruptly, his voice rang out, a magnificently dreadful baritone:

"I was down to Saint James' Infir-r-rmary," he sang. *"I saw my ba-a-aby there, stretched out on a long whi-i-ite ta-a-able—so sweet, so cold, so fair—"*

Moore swung his left hand, cross-body at the poet's midsection. He had plenty of target, but he was too slow. Unger blocked his fist and backed away, laughing.

Leota shook herself awake.

"What are you doing here?" she asked.

"Composing," he answered, "myself.

"Merry Christmas," he added.

"Go to hell," answered Moore.

"I congratulate you on your recent nuptials, Mister Moore."

"Thanks."

"Why wasn't I invited?"

"It was a simple ceremony."

He turned.

"Is that true, Leota? An old comrade-in-arms like me, not invited, just because it wasn't showy enough for my elaborate tastes?"

She nodded, fully awake now.

He struck his forehead.

"Oh, I am wounded!"

"Why don't you go back to wherever you came from?" asked Moore. "The drinks are on the house."

"I can't attend midnight mass in an inebriated condition."

Moore's fingers twitched back into fists.

"You may attend a mass for the dead without having to kneel."

"I believe you are hinting that you wish to be alone. I understand."

He withdrew to the rear of the Dart. After a time he began to snore.

"I hope we never see him again," she said.

"Why? He's a harmless drunk."

"No, he isn't. He hates us—because we're happy and he isn't."

"I think he's happiest when he's unhappy," smiled Moore, "and whenever the temperature drops. He loves the cold-bunk because it's like a little death to sleep in it. He once said, 'Each Setman dies many deaths. That's what I like about being a Setman.'

"You say more sleep won't be injurious—" he asked abruptly.

"No, there's no risk."

Below them, Time fled backward through the cold. Christmas was pushed out into the hallway and over the threshold of the front door to their world—Alvin's, Leota's, and Unger's world—to stand shivering on the doorsill of its own Eve, in Bermuda.

Inside the Dart, passing backward through Time, Moore recalled that New Year's Eve Party many years ago, recalled his desires of that day and reflected that they sat beside him now; recalled the Parties since then and reflected that he would miss all that were yet to come; recalled his work in the time before Time—a few months ago—and reflected that he could no longer do it properly—and that Time was indeed out of joint and that *he* could not set it aright; he recalled his old apartment, never revisited, all his old friends, including Diane Demetrios, now dead or senile, and reflected that, beyond the Set which he was leaving, he knew no one, save possibly the girl at his side. Only Wayne Unger was ageless, for he was an employee of the eternal. Given a month or two Unger could open up a bar, form his own circle of outcasts and toy with a private renaissance, if he should ever decide to leave.

Moore suddenly felt very stale and tired, and he whispered to their ghostly servant for a Martini and reached across his dozing wife to fetch it from the cubicle. He sat there sipping it, wondering about the world below.

He should have kept up with life, he decided. He knew nothing of contemporary politics, or law, or art; his standards were those grafted on by the Set, and concerned primarily with color, movement, gaiety, and clever speech; he was reduced again to childhood when it came to science. He knew he was wealthy, but the Set had been managing all his finances. All he had was an all-purpose card, good anywhere in the world for any sort of purchase, commodity or service-wise. Periodically, he had examined his file and seen balance sheets which told him he need never worry about being short of money. But he did not feel confident or competent when it came to meeting the people who resided in the world outside. Perhaps he would appear stodgy, old-fashioned, and "quaint" as he had felt tonight, without the glamor of the Set to mask his humanity.

Unger snored, Leota breathed deeply, and the world turned. When they reached Bermuda they returned to the Earth.

They stood beside the Dart, just outside the flight terminal.

"Care to take a walk?" asked Moore.

"I am tired, my love," said Leota, staring in the direction of the Hall of Sleep. She looked back.

He shook his head. "I'm not quite ready."

She turned to him. He kissed her.

"I'll see you then in April, darling. Good night."

"April is the cruelest month," observed Unger. "Come, engineer, I'll walk with you as far as the shuttle stands."

They began walking. They moved across the roadway in the direction opposite the terminal, and they entered upon the broad, canopied walk that led to the ro-car garage.

It was a crystalline night, with stars like tinsel and a satellite beacon blazing like a gold piece deep within the pool of the sky. As they walked, their breath fumed into white wreaths that vanished before they were fully formed. Moore tried in vain to light his pipe. Finally, he stopped and hunched his shoulders against the wind until he got it going.

"A good night for walking," said Unger.

Moore grunted. A gust of wind lashed a fiery rain of loose tobacco upon his cheek. He smoked on, hands in the pockets of his jacket, collar raised. The poet clapped him on the shoulder.

"Come with me into the town," he suggested. "It's only over the hill. We can walk it."

"No," said Moore, through his teeth.

They strode on, and as they neared the garage Unger grew uneasy.

"I'd rather someone were with me tonight," he said abruptly. "I feel strange, as though I'd drunk the draught of the centuries and suddenly am wise in a time when wisdom is unnecessary. I—I'm afraid."

Moore hesitated.

"No," he finally repeated, "it's time to say goodbye. You're traveling on and we're getting off. Have fun."

Neither offered to shake hands, and Moore watched him move into the shuttle stop.

Continuing behind the building, Moore cut diagonally across the wide lawns and into the garden. He strolled aimlessly for a few minutes, then found the path that led down to the ruins.

The going was slow and he wound his way through the cold wilderness. After a period of near-panic when he felt surrounded by trees and had had to backtrack, he emerged into the starlit clearing where menaces of shrubbery dappled the broken buildings with patterns of darkness, moving restlessly as the winds shifted.

The grass rustled about his ankles as he seated himself on a fallen pillar and got his pipe going once more.

He sat thinking himself into marble as his toes grew numb, and he felt very much a part of the place; an artificial scene, a ruin transplanted out of history onto unfamiliar grounds. He did not want to move. He just wanted to freeze into the landscape and become his own monument. He sat there making pacts with imaginary devils: he wanted to go back, to return with Leota to his Frisco town, to work again. Like Unger, he suddenly felt wise in time when wisdom was unnecessary. Knowledge was what he needed. Fear was what he had.

Pushed on by the wind, he picked his way across the plain. Within the circle of his fountain, Pan was either dead or sleeping. Perhaps it is the cold sleep of the gods, decided Moore, and Pan will one day awaken and blow upon his festival pipes and only the wind among high towers will answer, and the shuffling tread of an assessment robot be quickened to scan him—because the Party people will have forgotten the festival melodies, and the waxen ones will have isolated out the wisdom of the blood on their colored slides and inoculated mankind against it—and, programmed against emotions, a frivolity machine will perpetually generate the sensations of gaiety into the fever-dreams of the delirious, so that they will not recognize his tunes—and there shall be none among the children of Phoebus to even repeat the Attic cry of his first passing, heard those many Christmases ago beyond the waters of the Mediterranean.

Moore wished that he had stayed a little longer with Unger, because he now felt that he had gained a glimpse of the man's perspective. It had taken the fear of a new world to generate these feelings, but he was beginning to understand the poet. Why did the man stay on in the Set, though? he wondered. Did he take a masochistic pleasure in seeing his ice-prophecies fulfilled, as he moved further and further away from his own times? Maybe that was it.

Moore stirred himself into one last pilgrimage. He walked along their old path down to the breakwall. The stones were cold beneath his fingers, so he used the stile to cross over to the beach.

He stood on a rim of rust at the star-reflecting bucket-bottom of the world. He stared out at the black humps of the rocks where they had held their sunny colloquy days/months ago. It was his machines he had spoken of then, before they had spoken of themselves. He had believed, still believed, in their inevitable fusion with the spirit of his kind, into greater and finer vessels for life. Now he feared, like Unger, that by the time this occurred something else might have been lost, and that the fine new vessels would only be partly filled, lacking some essential ingredient. He hoped Unger was wrong; he felt that the ups and downs of Time might at some future equinox restore all those drowsing verities of the soul's undersides that he was now feeling—and that there *would* be ears to hear the piped melody, and feet that would move with its sound. He tried to believe this. He hoped it would be true.

A star fell, and Moore looked at his watch. It was late. He scuffed his way back to the wall and crossed over it again.

Inside the pre-sleep clinic he met Jameson, who was already yawning from his prep-injection. Jameson was a tall, thin man with the hair of a cherub and the eyes of its opposite number.

"Moore," he grinned, watching him hang his jacket on the wall and roll up his sleeve. "You going to spend your honeymoon on ice?"

The hypogun sighed in the medic's husky hand and the prep-injection entered Moore's arm.

"That's right," he replied, leveling his gaze at the not completely sober Jameson. "Why?"

"It just doesn't seem the thing to do," Jameson explained, still grinning. "If I were married to Leota you wouldn't catch me going on ice. Unless—"

Moore took one step toward him, the sound in his throat like a snarl. Jameson drew back, his dark eyes widening.

"I was joking!" he said. "I didn't . . ."

There was a pain in Moore's injected arm as the big medic seized it and jerked him to a halt.

"Yeah," said Moore, "good night. Sleep tight, wake sober."

As he turned toward the door the medic released his arm. Moore rolled down his sleeve and donned his jacket as he left.

"You're off your rocker," Jameson called after him.

Moore had about half an hour before he had to hit his bunker. He did not feel like heading for it at the moment. He had planned on waiting in the clinic until the injection began to work, but Jameson's presence changed that.

He walked through the wide corridors of the Hall of Sleep, rode a lift up to the bunkers, then strode down the hallway until he came to his door. He hesitated, then passed on. He would sleep there for the next three and a half months; he did not feel like giving it half of the next hour also.

He refilled his pipe. He would smoke through a sentinel watch beside the ice goddess, his wife. He looked about for wandering medics. One is supposed to refrain from smoking after the prep-injection, but it had never bothered him yet, or anyone else he knew of.

An intermittent thumping sound reached his ears as he moved on up the hallway. It stopped as he rounded a corner, then began again, louder. It was coming from up ahead.

After a moment there was another silence.

He paused outside Leota's door. Grinning around his pipe, he found a pen and drew a line through the last name on her plate. He printed "Moore" in above it. As he was forming the final letter the pounding began again.

It was coming from inside her room.

He opened the door, took a step, then stopped.

The man had his back to him. His right arm was raised. A mallet was clenched in his fist.

His panted mutterings, like an incantation, reached Moore's ears:

" 'Strew on her roses, roses, and never a spray of yew . . . In quiet she reposes—' "

Moore was across the chamber. He seized the mallet and managed to twist it away. Then he felt something break inside his hand as his fist connected with a jaw. The man collided with the opposite wall, then pitched forward onto the floor.

"Leota!" said Moore. "Leota..."

Cast of white Parian she lay, deep within the coils of the bunker. The canopy had been raised high overhead. Her flesh was already firm as stone—because there was no blood on her breast where the stake had been driven in. Only cracks and fissures, as in stone.

"No," said Moore.

The stake was a very hard synthowood—like cocobolo, or quebracho, or perhaps lignum vitae—still to be unsplintered....

"No," said Moore.

Her face had the relaxed expression of a dreamer, her hair was the color of aluminum. His ring was on her finger....

There was a murmuring in the corner of the room.

"Unger," he said flatly, "why—did—you—do it?"

The man sucked air around his words. His eyes were focused on something nameless.

"... Vampire," he muttered, "luring men aboard her Flying Dutchman to drain them across the years.... She is the future—a goddess on the outside and a thirsting vacuum within," he stated without emotion. "'Strew on her roses, roses... Her mirth the world required—She bathed it in smiles of glee...' She was going to leave me way up here in the middle of the air. I can't get off the merry-go-round and I can't have the brass ring. But no one else will lose as I have lost, not now. '... Her life was turning, turning, in mazes of heat and sound—' I thought she would come back to me, after she'd tired of you."

He raised his hands to cover his eyes as Moore advanced upon him.

"To the technician, the future—"

Moore hit him with the hammer, once, twice. After the third blow he lost count because his mind could not conceive of any number greater than three.

Then he was walking, running, the mallet still clutched in his hand—past doors like blind eyes, up corridors, down seldom-used stairwells.

As he lurched away from the Hall of Sleep he heard someone calling after him through the night. He kept running.

After a long while he began to walk again. His hand was aching and his breath burned within his lungs. He climbed a hill, paused at its top, then descended the other side.

Party Town, an expensive resort—owned and sponsored, though seldom patronized by the Set—was deserted, except for the Christmas lights in the windows, and the tinsel, and the boughs of holly. From some dim adytum the recorded carols of a private celebration could be heard, and some laughter. These things made Moore feel even more alone as he walked up one street and down another, his body seeming ever more a thing apart from him as the prep-injection took its inevitable effect. His feet were leaden. His eyes kept closing and he kept forcing them back open.

There were no services going on when he entered the church. It was warmer inside. He was alone there, too.

The interior of the church was dim, and he was attracted to an array of lights about the display at the foot of a statue. It was a manger scene. He leaned back against a pew and stared at the mother and the child, at the angels and the inquisitive cattle, at the father. Then he made a sound he had no words for and threw the mallet into the little stable and turned away. Clawing at the wall, he staggered off a dozen steps and collapsed, cursing and weeping, until he slept.

They found him at the foot of the cross.

Justice had become a thing of streamlined swiftness since the days of Moore's boyhood. The sheer force of world population had long ago crowded every docket of every court to impossible extremes, until measures were taken to waive as much of the paraphernalia as could be waived and hold court around the clock. That was why Moore faced judgment at ten o'clock in the evening, two days after Christmas.

The trial lasted less than a quarter of an hour. Moore waived representation; the charges were read; he entered a plea of guilty, and the judge sentenced him to death in the gas chamber without looking up from the stack of papers on his bench.

Numbly, Moore left the courtroom and was returned to a cell for his final meal, which he did not remember eating. He had no conception of the juridical process in this year in which he had come to rest. The Set attorney had simply looked bored as he told him his story, then mentioned "symbolic penalties" and told him to waive representation and enter a simple plea of "guilty to the homicide as described." He signed a statement to that effect. Then the attorney had left him and Moore had not spoken with anyone but his warders up until the time of the trial, and then only a few words before he went into court. And now—to receive a death sentence after he had admitted he was guilty of killing his wife's murderer —he could not conceive that justice had been done. Despite this, he felt an unnatural calm as he chewed mechanically upon whatever he had ordered. He was not afraid to die. He could not believe in it.

An hour later they came for him. He was led to a small, airtight room with a single, thick window set high in its metal door. He seated himself upon the bench within it and his gray-uniformed guards slammed the door behind him.

After an interminable time he heard the pellets breaking and he smelled the fumes. They grew stronger.

Finally, he was coughing and breathing fire and gasping and crying out, and he thought of her lying there in her bunker, the ironic strains of Unger's song during their Dart-flight recurring in his mind:

> *"I was down to Saint James' Infir-r-rmary.*
> *I saw my ba-a-aby there,*
> *Stretched out on a long white ta-a-able—*
> *So sweet, so cold, so fair . . ."*

Had Unger been consciously contemplating her murder even then? he wondered. Or was it something lurking below his consciousness? Something he had felt stirring, so that he had wanted Moore to stay with him—to keep it from happening?

He would never know, he realized, as the fires reached into his skull and consumed his brain.

As he awoke, feeling very weak upon white linen, the voice within his earphones was saying to Alvin Moore: ". . . Let that be a lesson to you."

Moore tore off the earphones with what he thought was a strong gesture, but his muscles responded weakly. Still, the earphones came off.

He opened his eyes and stared.

He might be in the Set's Sick Ward, located high up in the Hall of Sleep, or in hell. Franz Andrews, the attorney who had advised him to plead guilty, sat at his bedside.

"How do you feel?" he asked.

"Oh, great! Care to play a set of tennis?"

The man smiled faintly.

"You have successfully discharged your debt to

society," he stated, "through the symbolic penalty procedure."

"Oh, that explains everything," said Moore wryly. Finally: "I don't see why there had to be a penalty, symbolic or otherwise. That rhymer murdered my wife."

"He'll pay for it," said Andrews.

Moore rolled onto his side and studied the dispassionate flat-featured face at his elbow. The attorney's short hair was somewhere between blond and gray and his gaze unflinchingly sober.

"Do you mind repeating what you just said?"

"Not at all. I said he'd pay for it."

"He's not dead?"

"No, he's quite alive—two floors above us. His head has to heal before he can stand trial. He's too ill to face execution."

"He's alive!" said Moore. "Alive? Then what the hell was *I* executed for?"

"Well, you *did* kill the man," said Andrews, somewhat annoyed. "The fact that the doctors were later able to revive him does not alter the fact that a homicide occurred. The symbolic penalty exists for all such cases. You'll think twice before ever doing it again."

Moore tried to rise. He failed.

"Take it easy. You're going to need several more days of rest before you can get up. Your own revival was only last night."

Moore chuckled weakly. Then he laughed for a long, long time. He stopped, ending with a little sob.

"Feel better now?"

"Sure, sure," he whispered hoarsely. "Like a million bucks, or whatever the crazy currency is these days. What kind of execution will Unger get for murder?"

"Gas," said the attorney, "the same as you, if the alleged—"

"Symbolic, or for keeps?"

"Symbolic, of course."

Moore did not remember what happened next, except that he heard someone screaming and there was suddenly a medic whom he had not noticed doing something to his arm. He heard the soft hiss of an injection. Then he slept.

When he awakened he felt stronger and he noticed an insolent bar of sunlight streaking the wall opposite him. Andrews appeared not to have moved from his side.

He stared at the man and said nothing.

"I have been advised," said the attorney, "of your lack of knowledge concerning the present state of law in these matters. I did not stop to consider the length of your membership in the Set. These things so seldom occur—in fact, this is the first such case I've ever handled—that I simply assumed you knew what a symbolic penalty was when I spoke with you back in your cell. I apologize."

Moore nodded.

"Also," he continued, "I assumed that you had considered the circumstances under which Mister Unger allegedly committed a homicide—"

"'Allegedly,' hell! I was there. He drove a stake through her heart!" Moore's voice broke at that point.

"It *was* to have been a precedent-making decision," said Andrews, "as to whether he was to be indicted now for attempted homicide, or be detained until after the operation and face homicide charges if things do not go well. The matter of his detention then would have raised many more problems—which were fortunately resolved at his own suggestion. After his recovery he will retire to his bunker and remain there until the nature of the offense has been properly determined. He has volunteered to do this of his own free will, so no legal decision was delivered on the matter. His trial is postponed, there fore, until some of the surgical techniques have been refined—"

"What surgical techniques?" asked Moore, raising himself into a seated position and leaning against the headboard. His mind was fully alert for the first time since Christmas. He felt what was coming next.

He said one word.

"Explain."

Andrews shifted in his chair.

"Mister Unger," he began, "had a poet's conception as to the exact location of the human heart. He did not pierce it centrally, although the accidental angling of the stake did cause it to pass through the left ventricle. That can be repaired easily enough, according to the medics.

"Unfortunately, however, the slanting of the shaft caused it to strike against her spinal column," he said, "smashing two vertebrae and cracking several others. It appears that the spinal cord was severed. . . ."

Moore was numb again, numb with the realization that had dawned as the lawyer's words were filling the air between them. Of course she wasn't dead. Neither was she alive. She was sleeping the cold sleep. The spark of life would remain within her until the arousal began. *Then*, and only then, could she die. Unless—

" . . . Complicated by her pregnancy and the period of time necessary to raise her body temperature to an operable one," Andrews was saying.

"When are they going to operate?" Moore broke in.

"They can't say for certain, at this time," answered Andrews. "It will have to be a specially designed operation, as it raises problems for which there are answers in theory but not in practice. Any one of the factors could be treated at present, but the others couldn't be held in abeyance while the surgery is going on. Together, they are rather formidable—to repair the heart and fix the back, and to save the child, all at the same time, will require some new instrumentation and some new techniques."

"How long?" insisted Moore.

Andrews shrugged.

"They can't say. Months, years. She's all right as she is now, but—"

Moore asked him to go away, rather loudly, and he did.

The following day, feeling dizzy, he got to his feet and refused to return to bed until he could see Unger.

"He's in custody," said the medic who attended him.

"No he isn't," replied Moore. "You're not a lawyer, and I've already spoken with one. He won't be taken into legal custody until after he awakens from his next cold sleep—whenever that is."

It took over an hour for him to get permission to visit Unger. When he did, he was accompanied by Andrews and two orderlies.

"Don't you trust the symbolic penalty?" he smirked at Andrews. "You know that I'm supposed to think twice before I do it again."

Andrews looked away and did not answer him.

"Anyhow, I'm too weak and I don't have a hammer handy."

They knocked and entered.

Unger, his head turbaned in white, sat propped up by pillows. A closed book lay on the counterpane. He had been staring out of the window and into the garden. He turned his head toward them.

"Good morning, you son of a bitch," observed Moore.

"Please," said Unger.

Moore did not know what to say next. He had already expressed all that he felt. So he headed for the chair beside the bed and sat on it. He fished his pipe from the pocket of his robe and fumbled with it to hide his discomfort. Then he realized he had no tobacco with him. Neither Andrews nor the orderlies appeared to be watching them.

He placed the dry pipe between his teeth and looked up.

"I'm sorry," said Unger. "Can you believe that?"

"No," answered Moore.

"She's the future and she's yours," said Unger. "I drove a stake through her heart but she isn't really dead. They say they're working on the operating machines now. The doctors will fix up everything that I did, as good as new." He winced and looked down at the bedclothes.

"If it's any consolation to you," he continued, "I'm suffering and I'll suffer more. There is no Senta to save this Dutchman. I'm going to ride it out with the Set, or without it, in a bunker—die in some foreign place among strangers." He looked up, regarding Moore with a weak smile. Moore stared him back down. "They'll save her!" he insisted. "She'll sleep until they're absolutely certain of the technique. Then you two will get off together and I'll keep on going. You'll never see me after that. I wish you happiness. I won't ask your forgiveness."

Moore got to his feet.

"We've got nothing left to say. We'll talk again some year, in a day or so."

He left the room wondering what else he could have said.

"An ethical question has been put before the Set— that is to say, myself," said Mary Maude. "Unfortunately, it was posed by government attornies, so it cannot be treated as most ethical questions are to be treated. It requires an answer."

"Involving Moore and Unger?" asked Andrews.

"Not directly. Involving the entire Set, as a result of their escapade."

She indicated the fac-sheet on her desk. Andrews nodded.

" 'Unto Us a Babe is Born,' " she read, considering the photo of the prostrate Setman in the church. "A front-page editorial in this periodical has accused us of creating all varieties of neurotics—from necrophilists on down the line. Then there's that other photo—we still don't know who took it—here, on page three—"

"I've seen it."

"They now want assurances that ex-Setmen will remain frivolous and not turn into eminent undesirables."

"This is the first time it's ever happened—like this."

"Of course," she smiled. "They're usually decent enough to wait a few weeks before going anti-social—and wealth generally compensates for most normal maladjustments. But, according to the accusations, we are either selecting the wrong people—which is ridiculous—or not mustering them out properly when they leave—which is profoundly ridiculous. First, because I do all the interviewing, and second, because you *can't* boot a person half a century or so into the future and expect him to land on his feet as his normal, cheerful self, regardless of any orientation you may give him. Our people make a good show of it, though, because they don't generally do much of anything.

"But both Moore and Unger were reasonably normal, and they never knew each other particularly well. Both watched a little more closely than most Setmen as their worlds became history, and both were highly sensitive to those changes. Their problem, though, was interpersonal."

Andrews said nothing.

"By that, I mean it was a simple case of jealousy over a woman—an unpredictable human variable. I could not have foreseen their conflict. The changing times have nothing to do with it. Do they?"

Andrews did not answer.

"...Therefore, there is no problem," she continued. "We are not dumping Kaspar Hausers onto the street. We are simply transplanting wealthy people of good taste a few generations into the future—and they get on well. Our only misstep so far was predicated upon a male antagonism of the mutually accelerating variety, caused by a beautiful woman. That's all. Do you agree?"

"He thought that he was really going to die . . ." said Andrews. "I didn't stop to think that he knew nothing of the World Legal Code."

"A minor matter," she dismissed it. "He's still living."

"You should have seen his face when he came to in the Clinic."

"I'm not interested in faces. I've seen too many. Our problem now is to manufacture a problem and then to solve it to the government's satisfaction."

"The world changes so rapidly that I almost need to make a daily adjustment to it myself. These poor—"

"Some things do not change," said Mary Maude, "but I can see what you're driving at. Very clever. We'll hire us an independent Psych Team to do us a study indicating that what the Set needs is more adjustment, and they'll recommend that one day be set aside every year for therapeutic purposes. We'll hold each one in a different part of the world—at a non-Party locale. Lots of cities have been screaming for concessions. They'll all be days spent doing simple, adjustive things, mingling with un-Set people. Then, in the evening we'll have a light meal, followed by casual, restful entertainment, and then some dancing—dancing's good for the psyche, it relaxes tensions. I'm sure that will satisfy all parties concerned." She smiled at the last.

"I believe you are right," said Andrews.

"Of course. After the Psych Team writes several thousand pages, you'll draft a few hundred of your own to summarize the findings and cast them into the form of a resolution to be put before the board."

He nodded.

"I thank you for your suggestions."

"Any time. That's what I'm paid for."

After he had left, Mary Maude donned her black glove and placed another log on the fire. Genuine logs cost more and more every year, but she did not trust flameless heaters.

It was three days before Moore had recovered sufficiently to enter the sleep again. As the prep-injection dulled his senses and his eyes closed, he wondered what alien judgment day would confront him when he awakened. He knew, though, that whatever else the new year brought, his credit would be good.

He slept, and the world passed by.

THE DOORS OF HIS FACE,
THE LAMPS OF HIS MOUTH

I'm a baitman. No one is born a baitman, except in a French novel where everyone is. (In fact, I think that's the title, *We are All Bait*. Pfft!) How I got that way is barely worth the telling and has nothing to do with neo-exes, but the days of the beast deserve a few words, so here they are.

The Lowlands of Venus lie between the thumb and forefinger of the continent known as Hand. When you break into Cloud Alley it swings its silver-black bowling ball toward you without a warning. You jump then, inside that firetailed tenpin they ride you down in, but the straps keep you from making a fool of yourself. You generally chuckle afterwards, but you always jump first.

Next, you study Hand to lay its illusion and the two middle fingers become dozen-ringed archipelagoes as the outers resolve into green-gray peninsulas;

the thumb is too short, and curls like the embryo tail of Cape Horn.

You suck pure oxygen, sigh possibly, and begin the long topple to the Lowlands.

There, you are caught like an infield fly at the Lifeline landing area—so named because of its nearness to the great delta in the Eastern Bay—located between the first peninsula and "thumb." For a minute it seems as if you're going to miss Lifeline and wind up as canned seafood, but afterwards—shaking off the metaphors—you descend to scorched concrete and present your middle-sized telephone directory of authorizations to the short, fat man in the gray cap. The papers show that you are not subject to mysterious inner rottings and etcetera. He then smiles you a short, fat, gray smile and motions you toward the bus which hauls you to the Reception Area. At the R.A. you spend three days proving that, indeed, you are not subject to mysterious inner rottings and etcetera.

Boredom, however, is another rot. When your three days are up, you generally hit Lifeline hard, and it returns the compliment as a matter of reflex. The effects of alcohol in variant atmospheres is a subject on which the connoisseurs have written numerous volumes, so I will confine my remarks to noting that a good binge is worthy of at least a week's time and often warrants a lifetime study.

I had been a student of exceptional promise (strictly undergraduate) for going on two years when the *Bright Water* fell through our marble ceiling and poured its people like targets into the city.

Pause. The Worlds Almanac re Lifeline: ". . . Port city on the eastern coast of Hand. Employees of the Agency for Non-terrestrial Research comprise approximately 85% of its 100,000 population (2010 Census). Its other residents are primarily personnel maintained by several industrial corporations engaged in basic research. Independent marine biologists, wealthy fishing enthusiasts, and waterfront entrepreneurs make up the remainder of its inhabitants."

I turned to Mike Dabis, a fellow entrepreneur, and commented on the lousy state of basic research.

"Not if the mumbled truth be known."

He paused behind his glass before continuing the slow swallowing process calculated to obtain my interest and a few oaths, before he continued.

"Carl," he finally observed, poker playing, "they're shaping Tensquare."

I could have hit him. I might have refilled his glass with sulfuric acid and looked on with glee as his lips blackened and cracked. Instead, I grunted a noncommital.

"Who's fool enough to shell out fifty grand a day? ANR?"

He shook his head.

"Jean Luharich," he said, "the girl with the violet contacts and fifty or sixty perfect teeth. I understand her eyes are really brown."

"Isn't she selling enough face cream these days?"

He shrugged.

"Publicity makes the wheels go 'round. Luharich Enterprises jumped sixteen points when she picked up the Sun Trophy. You ever play golf on Mercury?"

I had, but I overlooked it and continued to press.

"So she's coming here with a blank check and a fishhook?"

"*Bright Water*, today," he nodded. "Should be down by now. Lots of cameras. She wants an Ikky, bad."

"Hmm," I hmmed. "How bad?"

"Sixty day contract, Tensquare. Indefinite extension clause. Million and a half deposit," he recited.

"You seem to know a lot about it."

"I'm Personnel Recruitment. Luharich Enterprises

approached me last month. It helps to drink in the right places.

"Or own them." He smirked, after a moment.

I looked away, sipping my bitter brew. After awhile I swallowed several things and asked Mike what he expected to be asked, leaving myself open for his monthly temperance lecture.

"They told me to try getting you," he mentioned. "When's the last time you sailed?"

"Month and a half ago. The *Corning*."

"Small stuff," he snorted. "When have you been under, yourself?"

"It's been awhile."

"It's been over a year, hasn't it? That time you got cut by the screw, under the *Dolphin?*"

I turned to him.

"I was in the river last week, up at Angleford where the currents are strong. I can still get around."

"Sober," he added.

"I'd stay that way," I said, "on a job like this."

A doubting nod.

"Straight union rates. Triple time for extraordinary circumstances," he narrated. "Be at Hangar Sixteen with your gear, Friday morning, 500 hours. We push off Saturday, daybreak."

"You're sailing?"

"I'm sailing."

"How come?"

"Money."

"Ikky guano."

"The bar isn't doing so well and baby needs new minks."

"I repeat—"

". . . And I want to get away from baby, renew my contact with basics—fresh air, exercise, make cash. . . ."

"All right, sorry I asked."

I poured him a drink, concentrating on H_2SO_4, but it didn't transmute. Finally I got him soused and went out into the night to walk and think things over.

Around a dozen serious attempts to land *Ichthyform Leviosaurus Levianthus,* generally known as "Ikky," had been made over the past five years. When Ikky was first sighted, whaling techniques were employed. These proved either fruitless or disastrous, and a new procedure was inaugurated. Tensquare was constructed by a wealthy sportsman named Michael Jandt, who blew his entire roll on the project.

After a year on the Eastern Ocean, he returned to file bankruptcy. Carlton Davits, a playboy fishing enthusiast, then purchased the huge raft and laid a wake for Ikky's spawning grounds. On the nineteenth day out he had a strike and lost 150 bills' worth of untested gear, along with one *Ichthy form Levianthus.* Twelve days later, using tripled lines, he hooked, narcotized, and began to hoist the huge beast. It awakened then, destroyed a control tower, killed six men, and worked general hell over five square blocks of Tensquare. Carlton was left with partial hemiplegia and a bankruptcy suit of his own. He faded into waterfront atmosphere and Tensquare changed hands four more times, with less spectacular but equally expensive results.

Finally, the big raft, built only for one purpose, was purchased at auction by ANR for "marine research." Lloyd's still won't insure it, and the only marine research it has ever seen is an occasional rental at fifty bills a day—to people anxious to tell Leviathan fish stories. I've been baitman on three of the voyages, and I've been close enough to count Ikky's fangs on two occasions. I want one of them to show my grandchildren, for personal reasons.

I faced the direction of the landing area and resolved a resolve.

"You want me for local coloring, gal. It'll look nice on the feature page and all that. But clear this— If anyone gets you an Ikky, it'll be me. I promise."

I stood in the empty Square. The foggy towers of Lifeline shared their mists.

Shoreline a couple eras ago, the western slope above Lifeline stretches as far as forty miles inland in some places. Its angle of rising is not a great one, but it achieves an elevation of several thousand feet before it meets the mountain range which separates us from the Highlands. About four miles inland and five hundred feet higher than Lifeline are set most of the surface airstrips and privately owned hangars. Hangar Sixteen houses Cal's Contract Cab, hop service, shore to ship. I do not like Cal, but he wasn't around when I climbed from the bus and waved to a mechanic.

Two of the hoppers tugged at the concrete, impatient beneath flywing haloes. The one on which Steve was working belched deep within its barrel carburetor and shuddered spasmodically.

"Bellyache?" I inquired.

"Yeah, gas pains and heartburn."

He twisted setscrews until it settled into an even keening, and turned to me.

"You're for out?"

I nodded.

"Tensquare. Cosmetics. Monsters. Stuff like that."

He blinked into the beacons and wiped his freckles. The temperature was about twenty, but the big overhead spots served a double purpose.

"Luharich," he muttered. "Then you *are* the one. There's some people want to see you."

"What about?"

"Cameras. Microphones. Stuff like that."

"I'd better stow my gear. Which one am I riding?"

He poked the screwdriver at the other hopper.

"That one. You're on video tape now, by the way. They wanted to get you arriving."

He turned to the hangar, turned back.

"Say 'cheese.' They'll shoot the close-ups later."

I said something other than "cheese." They must have been using telelens and been able to read my lips, because that part of the tape was never shown.

I threw my junk in the back, climbed into a passenger seat, and lit a cigarette. Five minutes later, Cal himself emerged from the office Quonset, looking cold. He came over and pounded on the side of the hopper. He jerked a thumb back at the hangar.

"They want you in there!" he called through cupped hands. "Interview!"

"The show's over!" I yelled back. "Either that, or they can get themselves another baitman!"

His rust-brown eyes became nailheads under blond brows and his glare a spike, before he jerked about and stalked off. I wondered how much they had paid him to be able to squat in his hangar and suck juice from his generator.

Enough, I guess, knowing Cal. I never liked the guy, anyway.

Venus at night is a field of sable waters. On the coasts, you can never tell where the sea ends and the sky begins. Dawn is like dumping milk into an inkwell. First, there are erratic curdles of white, then streamers. Shade the bottle for a gray colloid, then watch it whiten a little more. All of a sudden you've got day. Then start heating the mixture.

I had to shed my jacket as we flashed out over the bay. To our rear, the skyline could have been under water for the way it waved and rippled in the heatfall. A hopper can accommodate four people (five, if you want to bend Regs and underestimate weight), or three passengers with the sort of gear a baitman uses. I was the only fare, though, and the pilot was like his machine. He hummed and made no unnecessary noises. Lifeline turned a somersault and evaporated in the rear mirror at about the same time Tensquare broke the fore-horizon. The pilot stopped humming and shook his head.

I leaned forward. Feelings played flopdoodle in my guts. I knew every bloody inch of the big raft, but the feelings you once took for granted change when their source is out of reach. Truthfully, I'd had my doubts I'd ever board the hulk again. But now, now I could almost believe in predestination. There it was!

A tensquare football field of a ship. A-powered. Flat as a pancake, except for the plastic blisters in the middle and the "Rooks" fore and aft, port and starboard.

The Rook towers were named for their corner positions—and any two can work together to hoist, co-powering the graffles between them. The graffles—half-gaff, half-grapple—can raise enormous weights to near water level; their designer had only one thing in mind, though, which accounts for the gaff half. At water level, the Slider has to implement elevation for six to eight feet before the graffles are in a position to push upward, rather than pulling.

The Slider, essentially, is a mobile room—a big box capable of moving in any of Tensquare's crisscross groovings and "anchoring" on the strike side by means of a powerful electromagnetic bond. Its winches could hoist a battleship the necessary distance, and the whole craft would tilt, rather than the Slider come loose, if you want any idea of the strength of that bond.

The Slider houses a section operated control indicator which is the most sophisticated "reel" ever designed. Drawing broadcast power from the generator beside the center blister, it is connected by shortwave with the sonar room, where the movements of the quarry are recorded and repeated to the angler seated before the section control.

The fisherman might play his "lines" for hours, days even, without seeing any more than metal and an outline on the screen. Only when the beast is graffled and the extensor shelf, located twelve feet below waterline, slides out for support and begins to aid the winches, only then does the fisherman see his catch rising before him like a fallen seraph. Then, as Davits learned, one looks into the Abyss itself and is required to act. He didn't, and a hundred meters of unimaginable tonnage, undernarcotized and hurting, broke the cables of the winch, snapped a graffle, and took a half-minute walk across Tensquare.

We circled till the mechanical flag took notice and waved us on down. We touched beside the personnel hatch and I jettisoned my gear and jumped to the deck.

"Luck," called the pilot as the door was sliding shut. Then he danced into the air and the flag clicked blank.

I shouldered my stuff and went below.

Signing in with Malvern, the de facto captain, I learned that most of the others wouldn't arrive for a good eight hours. They had wanted me alone at Cal's so they could pattern the pub footage along twentieth-century cinema lines.

Open: landing strip, dark. One mechanic prodding a contrary hopper. Stark-o-vision shot of slow bus pulling in. Heavily dressed baitman descends, looks about, limps across field. Close-up: he grins. Move in for words: "Do you think this is the time? The time he *will* be landed?" Embarrassment, taciturnity, a shrug. Dub something—"I see. And why do you think Miss Luharich has a better chance than any of the others? Is it because she's better equipped?

(Grin.) Because more is known now about the creature's habits than when you were out before? Or is it because of her will to win, to be a champion? Is it any one of these things, or is it all of them?" Reply: "Yeah, all of them." "—Is that why you signed on with her? Because your instincts say, 'This one will be it'?" Answer: "She pays union rates. I couldn't rent that damned thing myself. And I want in." Erase. Dub something else. Fadeout as he moves toward hopper, etcetera.

"Cheese," I said, or something like that, and took a walk around Tensquare, by myself.

I mounted each Rook, checking out the controls and the underwater video eyes. Then I raised the main lift.

Malvern had no objections to my testing things this way. In fact, he encouraged it. We had sailed together before and our positions had even been reversed upon a time. So I wasn't surprised when I stepped off the lift into the Hopkins Locker and found him waiting. For the next ten minutes we inspected the big room in silence, walking through its copper coil chambers soon to be Arctic.

Finally, he slapped a wall.

"Well, will we fill it?"

I shook my head.

"I'd like to, but I doubt it. I don't give two hoots and a damn who gets credit for the catch, so long as I have a part in it. But it won't happen. That gal's an egomaniac. She'll want to operate the Slider, and she can't."

"You ever meet her?"

"Yeah."

"How long ago?"

"Four, five years."

"She was a kid then. How do you know what she can do now?"

"I know. She'll have learned every switch and

reading by this time. She'll be up on all theory. But do you remember one time we were together in the starboard Rook, forward, when Ikky broke water like a porpoise?"

"How could I forget?"

"Well?"

He rubbed his emery chin.

"Maybe she can do it, Carl. She's raced torch ships and she's scubaed in bad waters back home." He glanced in the direction of invisible Hand. "And she's hunted in the Highlands. She might be wild enough to pull that horror into her lap without flinching.

". . . For Johns Hopkins to foot the bill and shell out seven figures for the corpus," he added. "That's money, even to a Luharich."

I ducked through a hatchway.

"Maybe you're right, but she was a rich witch when I knew her.

"And she wasn't blonde," I added, meanly.

He yawned.

"Let's find breakfast."

We did that.

When I was young I thought that being born a sea creature was the finest choice Nature could make for anyone. I grew up on the Pacific coast and spent my summers on the Gulf or the Mediterranean. I lived months of my life negotiating coral, photographing trench dwellers, and playing tag with dolphins. I fished everywhere there are fish, resenting the fact that they can go places I can't. When I grew older I wanted bigger fish, and there was nothing living that I knew of, excepting a Sequoia, that came any bigger than Ikky. That's part of it. . . .

I jammed a couple of extra rolls into a paper bag and filled a thermos with coffee. Excusing myself, I left the galley and made my way to the Slider berth.

It was just the way I remembered it. I threw a few switches and the shortwave hummed.

"That you, Carl?"

"That's right, Mike. Let me have some juice down here, you double-crossing rat."

He thought it over, then I felt the hull vibrate as the generators cut in. I poured my third cup of coffee and found a cigarette.

"So why am I a double-crossing rat this time?" came his voice again.

"You knew about the cameramen at Hangar Sixteen?"

"Yes."

"Then you're a double-crossing rat. The last thing I want is publicity. 'He who fouled up so often before is ready to try it, nobly, once more.' I can read it now."

"You're wrong. The spotlight's only big enough for one, and she's prettier than you."

My next comment was cut off as I threw the elevator switch and the elephant ears flapped above me. I rose, settling flush with the deck. Retracting the lateral rail, I cut forward into the groove. Amidships, I stopped at a juncture, dropped the lateral, and retracted the longitudinal rail.

I slid starboard, midway between the Rooks, halted, and threw on the coupler.

I hadn't spilled a drop of coffee.

"Show me pictures."

The screen glowed. I adjusted and got outlines of the bottom.

"Okay."

I threw a Status Blue switch and he matched it. The light went on.

The winch unlocked. I aimed out over the waters, extended the arm, and fired a cast.

"Clean one," he commented.

"Status Red. Call strike." I threw a switch.

"Status Red."

The baitman would be on his way with this, to make the barbs tempting.

It's not exactly a fishhook. The cables bear hollow tubes; the tubes convey enough dope for any army of hopheads; Ikky takes the bait, dangled before him by remote control, and the fisherman rams the barbs home.

My hands moved over the console, making the necessary adjustments. I checked the narco-tank reading. Empty. Good, they hadn't been filled yet. I thumbed the Inject button.

"In the gullet," Mike murmured.

I released the cables. I played the beast imagined. I let him run, swinging the winch to simulate his sweep.

I had the air conditioner on and my shirt off and it was still uncomfortably hot, which is how I knew that morning had gone over into noon. I was dimly aware of the arrivals and departures of the hoppers. Some of the crew sat in the "shade" of the doors I had left open, watching the operation. I didn't see Jean arrive or I would have ended the session and gotten below.

She broke my concentration by slamming the door hard enough to shake the bond.

"Mind telling me who authorized you to bring up the Slider?" she asked.

"No one," I replied. "I'll take it below now."

"Just move aside."

I did, and she took my seat. She was wearing brown slacks and a baggy shirt and she had her hair pulled back in a practical manner. Her cheeks were flushed, but not necessarily from the heat. She attacked the panel with a nearly amusing intensity that I found disquieting.

"Status Blue," she snapped, breaking a violet fingernail on the toggle.

I forced a yawn and buttoned my shirt slowly. She

threw a side glance my way, checked the registers, and fired a cast.

I monitored the lead on the screen. She turned to me for a second.

"Status Red," she said levelly.

I nodded my agreement.

She worked the winch sideways to show she knew how. I didn't doubt she knew how and she didn't doubt that I didn't doubt, but then—

"In case you're wondering," she said, "you're not going to be anywhere near this thing. You were hired as a baitman, remember? Not a Slider operator! A baitman! Your duties consist of swimming out and setting the table for our friend the monster. It's dangerous, but you're getting well-paid for it. Any questions?"

She squashed the Inject button and I rubbed my throat.

"Nope," I smiled, "but I am qualified to run that thingamajigger—and if you need me I'll be available, at union rates."

"Mister Davits," she said, "I don't want a loser operating this panel."

"Miss Luharich, there has never been a winner at this game."

She started reeling in the cable and broke the bond at the same time, so that the whole Slider shook as the big yo-yo returned. We skidded a couple of feet backwards. She raised the laterals and we shot back along the groove. Slowing, she transferred rails and we jolted to a clanging halt, then shot off at a right angle. The crew scrambled away from the hatch as we skidded onto the elevator.

"In the future, Mister Davits, do not enter the Slider without being ordered," she told me.

"Don't worry. I won't even step inside if I am ordered," I answered. "I signed on as a baitman.

Remember? If you want me in here, you'll have to *ask* me."

"That'll be the day," she smiled.

I agreed, as the doors closed above us. We dropped the subject and headed in our different directions after the Slider came to a halt in its berth. She did say "good day," though, which I thought showed breeding as well as determination, in reply to my chuckle.

Later that night Mike and I stoked our pipes in Malvern's cabin. The winds were shuffling waves, and a steady spattering of rain and hail overhead turned the deck into a tin roof.

"Nasty," suggested Malvern.

I nodded. After two bourbons the room had become a familiar woodcut, with its mahogany furnishings (which I had transported from Earth long ago on a whim) and the dark walls, the seasoned face of Malvern, and the perpetually puzzled expression of Dabis set between the big pools of shadow that lay behind chairs and splashed in corners, all cast by the tiny table light and seen through a glass, brownly.

"Glad I'm in here."

"What's it like underneath on a night like this?"

I puffed, thinking of my light cutting through the insides of a black diamond, shaken slightly. The meteor-dart of a suddenly illuminated fish, the swaying of grotesque ferns, like nebulae—shadow, then green, then gone—swam in a moment through my mind. I guess it's like a spaceship would feel, if a spaceship could feel, crossing between worlds—and quiet, uncannily, preternaturally quiet; and peaceful as sleep.

"Dark," I said, "and not real choppy below a few fathoms."

"Another eight hours and we shove off," commented Mike.

"Ten, twelve days, we should be there," noted Malvern.

"What do you think Ikky's doing?"

"Sleeping on the bottom with Mrs. Ikky if he has any brains."

"He hasn't. I've seen ANR's skeletal extrapolation from the bones that have washed up—"

"Hasn't everyone?"

". . . Fully fleshed, he'd be over a hundred meters long. That right, Carl?"

I agreed.

". . . Not much of a brain box, though, for his bulk."

"Smart enough to stay out of our locker."

Chuckles, because nothing exists but this room, really. The world outside is an empty, sleet-drummed deck. We lean back and make clouds.

"Boss lady does not approve of unauthorized fly fishing."

"Boss lady can walk north till her hat floats."

"What did she say in there?"

"She told me that my place, with fish manure, is on the bottom."

"You don't Slide?"

"I bait."

"We'll see."

"That's all I do. If she wants a Slideman she's going to have to ask nicely."

"You think she'll have to?"

"I think she'll have to."

"And if she does, can you do it?"

"A fair question," I puffed. "I don't know the answer, though."

I'd incorporate my soul and trade 40 percent of the stock for the answer. I'd give a couple years off my life for the answer. But there doesn't seem to be a lineup of supernatural takers, because no one knows. Supposing when we get out there, luck being with us, we find ourselves an Ikky? Supposing we succeed in baiting him and get lines on him. What then? If we get him shipside, will she hold on or crack up? What if she's made of sterner stuff than Davits, who used to hunt sharks with poison-darted air pistols? Supposing she lands him and Davits has to stand there like a video extra.

Worse yet, supposing she asks for Davits and he still stands there like a video extra or something else—say, some yellow-bellied embodiment named Cringe?

It was when I got him up above the eight-foot horizon of steel and looked out at all that body, sloping on and on till it dropped out of sight like a green mountain range . . . And that head. Small for the body, but still immense. Fat, craggy, with lidless roulettes that had spun black and red since before my forefathers decided to try the New Continent. And swaying.

Fresh narco-tanks had been connected. It needed another shot, fast. But I was paralyzed.

It had made a noise like God playing a Hammond organ. . . .

And looked at me!

I don't know if seeing is even the same process in eyes like those. I doubt it. Maybe I was just a gray blur behind a black rock, with the plexi-reflected sky hurting its pupils. But it fixed on me. Perhaps the snake doesn't really paralyze the rabbit, perhaps it's just that rabbits are cowards by constitution. But it began to struggle and I still couldn't move, fascinated.

Fascinated by all that power, by those eyes, they found me there fifteen minutes later, a little broken about the head and shoulders, the Inject still unpushed.

And I dream about those eyes. I want to face them once more, even if their finding takes forever. I've got to know if there's something inside me that sets me apart from a rabbit, from notched plates of reflexes and instincts that always fall apart in exactly the same way whenever the proper combination is spun.

Looking down, I noticed that my hand was shaking. Glancing up, I noticed that no one else was noticing.

I finished my drink and emptied my pipe. It was late and no songbirds were singing.

I sat whittling, my legs hanging over the aft edge, the chips spinning down into the furrow of our wake. Three days out. No action.

"You!"

"Me?"

"You."

Hair like the end of the rainbow, eyes like nothing in nature, fine teeth.

"Hello."

"There's a safety rule against what you're doing, you know."

"I know. I've been worrying about it all morning."

A delicate curl climbed my knife, then drifted out behind us. It settled into the foam and was plowed under. I watched her reflection in my blade, taking a secret pleasure in its distortion.

"Are you baiting me?" she finally asked.

I heard her laugh then, and turned, knowing it had been intentional.

"What, me?"

"I could push you off from here, very easily."

"I'd make it back."

"Would you push me off, then—some dark night, perhaps?"

"They're all dark, Miss Luharich. No, I'd rather make you a gift of my carving."

She seated herself beside me then, and I couldn't help but notice the dimples in her knees. She wore white shorts and a halter and still had an offworld tan to her which was awfully appealing. I almost felt a twinge of guilt at having planned the whole scene, but my right hand still blocked her view of the wooden animal.

"Okay, I'll bite. What have you got for me?"

"Just a second. It's almost finished."

Solemnly, I passed her the wooden jackass I had been carving. I felt a little sorry and slightly jackass-ish myself, but I had to follow through. I always do. The mouth was split into a braying grin. The ears were upright.

She didn't smile and she didn't frown. She just studied it.

"It's very good," she finally said, "like most things you do—and appropriate, perhaps."

"Give it to me." I extended a palm.

She handed it back and I tossed it out over the water. It missed the white water and bobbed for awhile like a pigmy sea-horse.

"Why did you do that?"

"It was a poor joke. I'm sorry."

"Maybe you are right, though. Perhaps this time I've bitten off a little too much."

I snorted.

"Then why not do something safer, like another race?"

She shook her end of the rainbow.

"No. It has to be an Ikky."

"Why?"

"Why did you want one so badly that you threw away a fortune?"

"Many reasons," I said. "An unfrocked analyst who held black therapy sessions in his basement once told me, 'Mister Davits, you need to reinforce the image of your masculinity by catching one of every kind of fish in existence.' Fish are a very ancient masculinity symbol, you know. So I set out to do it. I have one more to go. Why do you want to reinforce *your* masculinity?"

"I don't," she said. "I don't want to reinforce anything but Luharich Enterprises. My chief statistician once said, 'Miss Luharich, sell all the cold cream and face powder in the System and you'll be a happy girl. Rich, too.' And he was right. I am the proof. I can look the way I do and do anything, and I sell most of the lipstick and face powder in the System—but I have to be *able* to do anything."

"You do look cool and efficient," I observed.

"I don't feel cool," she said, rising. "Let's go for a swim."

"May I point out that we are making pretty good time?"

"If you want to indicate the obvious, you may. You said you could make it back to the ship, unassisted. Change your mind?"

"No."

"Then get us two scuba outfits and I'll race you under Tensquare.

"I'll win, too," she added.

I stood and looked down at her, because that usually makes me feel superior to women.

"Daughter of Lir, eyes of Picasso," I said, "you've got yourself a race. Meet me at the forward Rook, starboard, in ten minutes."

"Ten minutes," she agreed.

And ten minutes it was. From the center blister to the Rook took maybe two of them, with the load I was carrying. My sandals grew very hot and I was glad to shuck them for flippers when I reached the comparative cool of the corner.

We slid into harnesses and adjusted our gear. She had changed into a trim one-piece green job that made me shade my eyes and look away, then look back again.

I fastened a rope ladder and kicked it over the side. Then I pounded on the wall of the Rook.

"Yeah?"

"You talk to the port Rook, aft?" I called.

"They're all set up," came the answer. "There's ladders and draglines all over that end."

"You sure you want to do this?" asked the sunburnt little gink who was her publicity man, Anderson yclept.

He sat beside the Rook in a deck chair, sipping lemonade through a straw.

"It might be dangerous," he observed, sunkenmouthed. (His teeth were beside him, in another glass.)

"That's right," she smiled. "It *will* be dangerous. Not overly, though."

"Then why don't you let me get some pictures? We'd have them back to Lifeline in an hour. They'd be in New York by tonight. Good copy."

"No," she said, and turned away from both of us.

She raised her hands to her eyes.

"Here, keep these for me."

She passed him a box full of her unseeing, and when she turned back to me they were the same brown that I remembered.

"Ready?"

"No," I said, tautly. "Listen carefully, Jean. If you're going to play this game, there are a few rules. First," I counted, "we're going to be directly beneath the hull, so we have to start low and keep moving. If we bump the bottom, we could rupture an air tank. . . ."

She began to protest that any moron knew that and I cut her down.

"Second," I went on, "there won't be much light, so we'll stay close together, and we will *both* carry torches."

Her wet eyes flashed.

"I dragged you out of Govino without—"

Then she stopped and turned away. She picked up a lamp.

"Okay. Torches. Sorry."

". . . And watch out for the drive-screws," I finished. "There'll be strong currents for at least fifty meters behind them."

She wiped her eyes again and adjusted the mask.

"All right, let's go."

We went.

She led the way, at my insistence. The surface layer was pleasantly warm. At two fathoms the water was bracing; at five it was nice and cold. At eight we let go the swinging stairway and struck out. Tensquare sped forward and we raced in the opposite direction, tattooing the hull yellow at ten-second intervals.

The hull stayed where it belonged, but we raced on like two darkside satellites. Periodically, I tickled her frog feet with my light and traced her antennae of bubbles. About a five-meter lead was fine; I'd beat her in the home stretch, but I couldn't let her drop behind yet.

Beneath us, black. Immense. Deep. The Mindanao of Venus, where eternity might eventually pass the dead to a rest in cities of unnamed fishes. I twisted my head away and touched the hull with a feeler of light; it told me we were about a quarter of the way along.

I increased my beat to match her stepped-up stroke, and narrowed the distance which she had suddenly opened by a couple meters. She sped up again and I did, too. I spotted her with my beam.

She turned and it caught on her mask. I never knew whether she'd been smiling. Probably. She raised two fingers in a V-for-Victory and then cut ahead at full speed.

I should have known. I should have felt it coming.

It was just a race to her, something else to win. Damn the torpedoes!

So I leaned into it, hard. I don't shake in the water. Or, if I do it doesn't matter and I don't notice it. I began to close the gap again.

She looked back, sped on, looked back. Each time she looked it was nearer, until I'd narrowed it down to the original five meters.

Then she hit the jatoes.

That's what I had been fearing. We were about halfway under and she shouldn't have done it. The powerful jets of compressed air could easily rocket her upward into the hull, or tear something loose if she allowed her body to twist. Their main use is in tearing free from marine plants or fighting bad currents. I had wanted them along as a safety measure, because of the big suck-and-pull windmills behind.

She shot ahead like a meteorite, and I could feel a sudden tingle of perspiration leaping to meet and mix with the churning waters.

I swept ahead, not wanting to use my own guns, and she tripled, quadrupled the margin.

The jets died and she was still on course. Okay, I was an old fuddy-duddy. She *could* have messed up and headed toward the top.

I plowed the sea and began to gather back my yardage, a foot at a time. I wouldn't be able to catch her or beat her now, but I'd be on the ropes before she hit deck.

Then the spinning magnets began their insistence and she wavered. It was an awfully powerful drag, even at this distance. The call of the meat grinder.

I'd been scratched up by one once, under the *Dolphin*, a fishing boat of the middle-class. I *had* been drinking, but it was also a rough day, and the thing had been turned on prematurely. Fortunately, it was turned off in time, also, and a tendon-stapler made everything good as new, except in the log, where it only mentioned that I'd been drinking. Nothing about it being off-hours when I had a right to do as I damn well pleased.

She had slowed to half her speed, but she was still moving crosswise, toward the port, aft corner. I began to feel the pull myself and had to slow down. She'd made it past the main one, but she seemed too far back. It's hard to gauge distances underwater, but each red beat of time told me I was right. She was out of danger from the main one, but the smaller port screw, located about eighty meters in, was no longer a threat but a certainty.

She had turned and was pulling away from it now. Twenty meters separated us. She was standing still. Fifteen.

Slowly, she began a backward drifting. I hit my jatoes, aiming two meters behind her and about twenty back of the blades.

Straightline! Thankgod! Catching, softbelly, leadpipe on shoulder SWIMLIKEHELL! maskcracked, not broke though AND UP!

We caught a line and I remember brandy.

Into the cradle endlessly rocking I spit, pacing. Insomnia tonight and left shoulder sore again, so let it rain on me—they can cure rheumatism. Stupid as hell. What I said. In blankets and shivering. She: "Carl, I can't say it." Me: "Then call it square for that night in Govino, Miss Luharich. Huh?" She: nothing. Me: "Any more of that brandy?" She: "Give me another, too." Me: sounds of sipping. It had only lasted three months. No alimony. Many $ on both sides. Not sure whether they were happy or not. Wine-dark Aegean. Good fishing. Maybe he should have spent more time on shore. Or perhaps she shouldn't have. Good swimmer, though. Dragged him all the way to Vido to wring out his lungs. Young. Both. Strong. Both. Rich and spoiled as hell.

Ditto. Corfu should have brought them closer. Didn't. I think that mental cruelty was a trout. He wanted to go to Canada. She: "Go to hell if you want!" He: "Will you go along?" She: "No." But she did, anyhow. Many hells. Expensive. He lost a monster or two. She inherited a couple. Lot of lightning tonight. Stupid as hell. Civility's the coffin of a conned soul. By whom?—Sounds like a bloody neo-ex. . . . But I hate you, Anderson, with your glass full of teeth and her new eyes. . . . Can't keep this pipe lit, keep sucking tobacco. Spit again!

Seven days out and the scope showed Ikky.

Bells jangled, feet pounded, and some optimist set the thermostat in the Hopkins. Malvern wanted me to sit it out, but I slipped into my harness and waited for whatever came. The bruise looked worse than it felt. I had exercised every day and the shoulder hadn't stiffened on me.

A thousand meters ahead and thirty fathoms deep, it tunneled our path. Nothing showed on the surface.

"Will we chase him?" asked an excited crewman.

"Not unless she feels like using money for fuel." I shrugged.

Soon the scope was clear, and it stayed that way. We remained on alert and held our course.

I hadn't said over a dozen words to my boss since the last time we went drowning together, so I decided to raise the score.

"Good afternoon," I approached. "What's new?"

"He's going north-northeast. We'll have to let this one go. A few more days and we can afford some chasing. Not yet."

Sleek head . . .

I nodded. "No telling where this one's headed."

"How's your shoulder?"

"All right. How about you?"

Daughter of Lir . . .

"Fine. By the way, you're down for a nice bonus."
Eyes of perdition!
"Don't mention it," I told her back.

Later that afternoon, and appropriately, a storm shattered. (I prefer "shattered" to "broke." It gives a more accurate idea of the behavior of tropical storms on Venus and saves lots of words.) Remember that inkwell I mentioned earlier? Now take it between thumb and forefinger and hit its side with a hammer. Watch yourself! Don't get splashed or cut—

Dry, then drenched. The sky one million bright fractures as the hammer falls. And sounds of breaking.

"Everyone below?" suggested loudspeakers to the already scurrying crew.

Where was I? Who do you think was doing the loudspeaking?

Everything loose went overboard when the water got to walking, but by then no people were loose. The Slider was the first thing below decks. Then the big lifts lowered their shacks.

I had hit it for the nearest Rook with a yell the moment I recognized the pre-brightening of the holocaust. From there I cut in the speakers and spent half a minute coaching the track team.

Minor injuries had occurred, Mike told me over the radio, but nothing serious. I, however, was marooned for the duration. The Rooks do not lead anywhere; they're set too far out over the hull to provide entry downwards, what with the extensor shelves below.

So I undressed myself of the tanks which I had worn for the past several hours, crossed my flippers on the table, and leaned back to watch the hurricane. The top was black as the bottom and we were in between, and somewhat illuminated because of all that flat, shiny space. The waters above didn't rain down—they just sort of got together and dropped.

The Rooks were secure enough—they'd weathered

any number of these onslaughts—it's just that their positions gave them a greater arc of rise and descent when Tensquare makes like the rocker of a very nervous grandma. I had used the belts from my rig to strap myself into the bolted-down chair, and I removed several years in purgatory from the soul of whoever left a pack of cigarettes in the table drawer.

I watched the water make teepees and mountains and hands and trees until I started seeing faces and people. So I called Mike.

"What are you doing down there?"

"Wondering what you're doing up there," he replied. "What's it like?"

"You're from the Midwest, aren't you?"

"Yeah."

"Get bad storms out there?"

"Sometimes."

"Try to think of the worst one you were ever in. Got a slide rule handy?"

"Right here."

"Then put a one under it, imagine a zero or two following after, and multiply the thing out."

"I can't imagine the zeros."

"Then retain the multiplicand—that's all you can do."

"So what are you doing up there?"

"I've strapped myself in the chair. I'm watching things roll around the floor right now."

I looked up and out again. I saw one darker shadow in the forest.

"Are you praying or swearing?"

"Damned if I know. But if this were the Slider—if only this were the Slider!"

"*He's out there?*"

I nodded, forgetting that he couldn't see me.

Big, as I remembered him. He'd only broken surface for a few moments, to look around. *There is no power on Earth that can be compared with him who was made to fear no one.* I dropped my cigarette. It was the same as before. Paralysis and an unborn scream.

"You all right, Carl?"

He had looked at me again. Or seemed to. Perhaps that mindless brute had been waiting half a millennium to ruin the life of a member of the most highly developed species in business. . . .

"You okay?"

. . . Or perhaps it had been ruined already, long before their encounter, and theirs was just a meeting of beasts, the stronger bumping the weaker aside, body to psyche. . . .

"Carl, dammit! Say something!"

He broke again, this time nearer. Did you ever see the trunk of a tornado? It seems like something alive, moving around in all that dark. Nothing has a right to be so big, so strong, and moving. It's a sickening sensation.

"Please answer me."

He was gone and did not come back that day. I finally made a couple of wisecracks at Mike, but I held my next cigarette in my right hand.

The next seventy or eighty thousand waves broke by with a monotonous similarity. The five days that held them were also without distinction. The morning of the thirteenth day out, though, our luck began to rise. The bells broke our coffee-drenched lethargy into small pieces, and we dashed from the galley without hearing what might have been Mike's finest punch line.

"Aft!" cried someone. "Five hundred meters!"

I stripped to my trunks and started buckling. My stuff is always within grabbing distance.

I flipflopped across the deck, girding myself with a deflated squiggler.

"Five hundred meters, twenty fathoms!" boomed the speakers.

The big traps banged upward and the Slider grew to its full height, m'lady at the console. It rattled past me and took root ahead. Its one arm rose and lengthened.

I breasted the Slider as the speakers called, "Four-eighty, twenty!"

"Status Red!"

A belch like an emerging champagne cork and the line arced high over the waters.

"Four-eighty, twenty!" it repeated, all Malvern and static. "Baitman, attend!"

I adjusted my mask and hand-over-handed it down the side. Then warm, then cool, then away.

Green, vast, down. Fast. This is the place where I am equal to a squiggler. If something big decides a baitman looks tastier than what he's carrying, then irony colors his title as well as the water about it.

I caught sight of the drifting cables and followed them down. Green to dark green to black. It had been a long cast, too long. I'd never had to follow one this far down before. I didn't want to switch on my torch.

But I had to.

Bad! I still had a long way to go. I clenched my teeth and stuffed my imagination into a straight jacket.

Finally the line came to an end.

I wrapped one arm about it and unfastened the squiggler. I attached it, working as fast as I could, and plugged in the little insulated connections which are the reason it can't be fired with the line. Ikky could break them, but by then it wouldn't matter.

My mechanical eel hooked up, I pulled its section plugs and watched it grow. I had been dragged deeper during this operation, which took about a minute and a half. I was near—too near—to where I never wanted to be.

Loathe as I had been to turn on my light, I was suddenly afraid to turn it off. Panic gripped me and I seized the cable with both hands. The squiggler began to glow, pinkly. It started to twist. It was twice as big as I am and doubtless twice as attractive to pink squiggler-eaters. I told myself this until I believed it, then I switched off my light and started up.

If I bumped into something enormous and steelhided my heart had orders to stop beating immediately and release me—to dart fitfully forever along Acheron, and gibbering.

Ungibbering, I made it to green water and fled back to the nest.

As soon as they hauled me aboard I made my mask a necklace, shaded my eyes, and monitored for surface turbulence. My first question, of course, was: "Where is he?"

"Nowhere," said a crewman; "we lost him right after you went over. Can't pick him up on the scope now. Musta dived."

"Too bad."

The squiggler stayed down, enjoying its bath. My job ended for the time being, I headed back to warm my coffee with rum.

From behind me, a whisper: "Could you laugh like that afterwards?"

Perceptive Answer: "Depends on what he's laughing at."

Still chuckling, I made my way into the center blister with two cupfuls.

"Still hell and gone?"

Mike nodded. His big hands were shaking, and mine were steady as a surgeon's when I set down the cups.

He jumped as I shrugged off the tanks and looked for a bench.

"Don't drip on that panel! You want to kill yourself and blow expensive fuses?"

I toweled down, then settled down to watching the unfilled eye on the wall. I yawned happily; my shoulder seemed good as new.

The little box that people talk through wanted to say something, so Mike lifted the switch and told it to go ahead.

"Is Carl there, Mister Dabis?"

"Yes, ma'am."

"Then let me talk to him."

Mike motioned and I moved.

"Talk," I said.

"Are you all right?"

"Yes, thanks. Shouldn't I be?"

"That was a long swim. I—I guess I overshot my cast."

"I'm happy," I said. "More triple-time for me. I really clean up on that hazardous duty clause."

"I'll be more careful next time," she apologized. "I guess I was too eager. Sorry—" Something happened to the sentence, so she ended it there, leaving me with half a bagful of replies I'd been saving.

I lifted the cigarette from behind Mike's ear and got a light from the one in the ashtray.

"Carl, she was being nice," he said, after turning to study the panels.

"I know," I told him. "I wasn't."

"I mean, she's an awfully pretty kid, pleasant. Headstrong and all that. But what's she done to you?"

"Lately?" I asked.

He looked at me, then dropped his eyes to his cup.

"I know it's none of my bus—" he began.

"Cream and sugar?"

Ikky didn't return that day, or that night. We picked up some Dixieland out of Lifeline and let the muskrat ramble while Jean had her supper sent to the Slider. Later she had a bunk assembled inside. I piped in "Deep Water Blues" when it came over the air and waited for her to call up and cuss us out. She didn't, though, so I decided she was sleeping.

Then I got Mike interested in a game of chess that went on until daylight. It limited conversation to several "checks," one "checkmate," and a "damn!" Since he's a poor loser it also effectively sabotaged subsequent talk, which was fine with me. I had a steak and fried potatoes for breakfast and went to bed.

Ten hours later someone shook me awake and I propped myself on one elbow, refusing to open my eyes.

"Whassamadder?"

"I'm sorry to get you up," said one of the younger crewmen, "but Miss Luharich wants you to disconnect the squiggler so we can move on."

I knuckled open one eye, still deciding whether I should be amused.

"Have it hauled to the side. Anyone can disconnect it."

"It's at the side now, sir. But she said it's in your contract and we'd better do things right."

"That's very considerate of her. I'm sure my Local appreciates her remembering."

"Uh, she also said to tell you to change your trunks and comb your hair, and shave, too. Mister Anderson's going to film it."

"Okay. Run along; tell her I'm on my way—and ask if she has some toenail polish I can borrow."

I'll save on details. It took three minutes in all, and I played it properly, even pardoning myself when I slipped and bumped into Anderson's white tropicals with the wet squiggler. He smiled, brushed it off; she smiled, even though Luharich Complectacolor couldn't completely mask the dark circles under her eyes; and I smiled, waving to all our fans out there in videoland. —Remember, Mrs. Universe, you, too, can look like a monster-catcher. Just use Luharich face cream.

I went below and made myself a tuna sandwich, with mayonnaise.

Two days like icebergs—bleak, blank, half-melting, all frigid, mainly out of sight, and definitely a threat to peace of mind—drifted by and were good to put behind. I experienced some old guilt feelings and had a few is disturbing dreams. Then I called Lifeline and checked my bank balance.

"Going shopping?" asked Mike, who had put the call through for me.

"Going home," I answered.

"Huh?"

"I'm out of the baiting business after this one, Mike. The Devil with Ikky! The Devil with Venus and Luharich Enterprises! And the Devil with you!"

Up eyebrows.

"What brought that on?"

"I waited over a year for this job. Now that I'm here, I've decided the whole thing stinks."

"You knew what it was when you signed on. No matter what else you're doing, you're selling face cream when you work for face-cream sellers."

"Oh, that's not what's biting me. I admit the commercial angle irritates me, but Tensquare has always been a publicity spot, ever since the first time it sailed."

"What, then?"

"Five or six things, all added up. The main one being that I don't care any more. Once it meant more to me than anything else to hook that critter, and now it doesn't. I went broke on what started out as a lark and I wanted blood for what it cost me. Now I realize that maybe I had it coming. I'm beginning to feel sorry for Ikky."

"And you don't want him now?"

"I'll take him if he comes peacefully, but I don't feel like sticking out my neck to make him crawl into the Hopkins."

"I'm inclined to think it's one of the four or five other things you said you added."

"Such as?"

He scrutinized the ceiling.

I growled.

"Okay, but I won't say it, not just to make you happy you guessed right."

He, smirking: "That look she wears isn't just for Ikky."

"No good, no good." I shook my head. "We're both fission chambers by nature. You can't have jets on both ends of the rocket and expect to go anywhere —what's in the middle just gets smashed."

"That's how it *was*. None of my business, of course—"

"Say that again and you'll say it without teeth."

"Any day, big man"—he looked up—"any place . . ."

"So go ahead. Get it said!"

"She doesn't care about that bloody reptile, she came here to drag you back where you belong. You're not the baitman this trip."

"Five years is too long."

"There must be something under that cruddy hide of yours that people like," he muttered, "or I wouldn't be talking like this. Maybe you remind us humans of some really ugly dog we felt sorry for when we were kids. Anyhow, someone wants to take you home and raise you—also, something about beggars not getting menus."

"Buddy," I chuckled, "do you know what I'm going to do when I hit Lifeline?"

"I can guess."

"You're wrong. I'm torching it to Mars, and then I'll cruise back home, first class. Venus bankruptcy provisions do not apply to Martian trust funds, and I've still got a wad tucked away where moth and corruption enter not. I'm going to pick up a big old mansion on the Gulf and if you're ever looking for a job you can stop around and open bottles for me."

"You are a yellow-bellied fink," he commented.

"Okay," I admitted, "but it's her I'm thinking of, too."

"I've heard the stories about you both," he said. "So you're a heel and a goof-off and she's a bitch. That's called compatibility these days. I dare you, baitman, try keeping something you catch."

I turned.

"If you ever want that job, look me up."

I closed the door quietly behind me and left him sitting there waiting for it to slam.

The day of the beast dawned like any other. Two days after my gutless flight from empty waters I went down to rebait. Nothing on the scope. I was just making things ready for the routine attempt.

I hollered a "good morning" from outside the Slider and received an answer from inside before I pushed off. I had reappraised Mike's words, sans sound, sans fury, and while I did not approve of their sentiment or significance, I had opted for civility anyhow.

So down, under, and away. I followed a decent cast about 290 meters out. The snaking cables burned black to my left and I paced their undulations from the yellow-green down into the darkness. Soundless lay the wet night, and I bent my way through it like a cockeyed comet, bright tail before.

I caught the line, slick and smooth, and began baiting. An icy world swept by me then, ankles to head. It was a draft, as if someone had opened a big door beneath me. I wasn't drifting downwards that fast either.

Which meant that something might be moving up, something big enough to displace a lot of water. I still didn't think it was Ikky. A freak current of some sort, but not Ikky. Ha!

I had finished attaching the leads and pulled the first plug when a big, rugged, black island grew beneath me....

I flicked the beam downward. His mouth was opened.

I was rabbit.

Waves of the death-fear passed downward. My stomach imploded. I grew dizzy.

Only one thing, and one thing only, left to do. I managed it, finally. I pulled the rest of the plugs.

I could count the scaly articulations ridging his eyes by then.

The squiggler grew, pinked into phosphorescence ... squiggled!

Then my lamp. I had to kill it, leaving just the bait before him.

One glance back as I jammed the jatoes to life.

He was so near that the squiggler reflected on his teeth, in his eyes. Four meters, and I kissed his lambent jowls with two jets of backwash as I soared. Then I didn't know whether he was following or had halted. I began to black out as I waited to be eaten.

The jatoes died and I kicked weakly.

Too fast, I felt a cramp coming on. One flick of the beam, cried rabbit. One second, to know ...

Or end things up, I answered. No, rabbit, we don't dart before hunters. Stay dark.

Green waters finally, to yellow-green, then top.

Doubling, I beat off toward Tensquare. The waves from the explosion behind pushed me on ahead. The world closed in, and I screamed, "He's alive!" in the distance.

A giant shadow and a shock wave. The line was alive, too. Happy Fishing Grounds. Maybe I did something wrong....

Somewhere hand was clenched. What's bait?

* * *

A few million years. I remember starting out as a one-celled organism and painfully becoming an amphibian, then an air-breather. From somewhere high in the treetops I heard a voice.

"He's coming around."

I evolved back into homosapience, then a step further into a hangover.

"Don't try to get up yet."

"Have we got him?" I slurred.

"Still fighting, but he's hooked. We thought he took you for an appetizer."

"So did I."

"Breathe some of this and shut up."

A funnel over my face. Good. Lift your cups and drink. . . .

"He was awfully deep. Below scope range. We didn't catch him till he started up. Too late, then."

I began to yawn.

"We'll get you inside now."

I managed to uncase my ankle knife.

"Try it and you'll be minus a thumb."

"You need rest."

"Then bring me a couple more blankets. I'm staying."

I fell back and closed my eyes.

Someone was shaking me. Gloom and cold. Spotlights bled yellow on the deck. I was in a jury-rigged bunk, bulked against the center blister. Swaddled in wool, I still shivered.

"It's been eleven hours. You're not going to see anything now."

I tasted blood.

"Drink this."

Water. I had a remark but I couldn't mouth it.

"Don't ask how I feel," I croaked. "I know that comes next, but don't ask me. Okay?"

"Okay. Want to go below now?"

"No. Just get me my jacket."

"Right here."

"What's he doing?"

"Nothing. He's deep, he's doped but he's staying down."

"How long since last time he showed?"

"Two hours, about."

"Jean?"

"She won't let anyone in the Slider. Listen, Mike says come on in. He's right behind you in the blister."

I sat up and turned. Mike was watching. He gestured; I gestured back.

I swung my feet over the edge and took a couple of deep breaths. Pains in my stomach. I got to my feet and made it into the blister.

"Howza gut?" queried Mike.

I checked the scope. No Ikky. Too deep.

"You buying?"

"Yeah, coffee."

"Not coffee."

"You're ill. Also, coffee is all that's allowed in here."

"Coffee is a brownish liquid that burns your stomach. You have some in the bottom drawer."

"No cups. You'll have to use a glass."

"Tough."

He poured.

"You do that well. Been practicing for that job?"

"What job?"

"The one I offered you—"

A blot on the scope!

"Rising, ma'am! Rising!" he yelled into the box.

"Thanks, Mike. I've got it in here," she crackled.

"Jean!"

"Shut up! She's busy!"

"Was that Carl?"

"Yeah," I called. "Talk later," and I cut it.

Why did I do that?

"Why did you do that?"
I didn't know.
"I don't know."
Damned echoes! I got up and walked outside.
Nothing. Nothing.
Something?

Tensquare actually rocked! He must have turned when he saw the hull and started downward again. White water to my left, and boiling. An endless spaghetti of cable roared hotly into the belly of the deep.

I stood awhile, then turned and went back inside.
Two hours sick. Four, and better.
"The dope's getting to him."
"Yeah."
"What about Miss Luharich?"
"What about her?"
"She must be half dead."
"Probably."
"What are you going to do about it?"
"She signed the contract for this. She knew what might happen. It did."
"I think you could land him."
"So do I."
"So does she."
"Then let her ask me."

Ikky was drafting lethargically, at thirty fathoms.

I took another walk and happened to pass behind the Slider. She wasn't looking my way.

"Carl, come in here!"

Eyes of Picasso, that's what, and a conspiracy to make me Slide . . .

"Is that an order?"
"Yes—No! Please."

I dashed inside and monitored. He was rising.
"Push or pull?"

I slammed the "wind" and he came like a kitten.
"Make up your own mind now."

He balked at ten fathoms.

"Play him?"

"No!"

She wound him upwards—five fathoms, four . . .

She hit the extensors at two, and they caught him. Then the graffles.

Cries without and a heat lightning of flashbulbs.

The crew saw Ikky.

He began to struggle. She kept the cables tight, raised the graffles . . .

Up.

Another two feet and the graffles began pushing.

Screams and fast footfalls.

Giant beanstalk in the wind, his neck, waving. The green hills of his shoulders grew.

"He's big, Carl!" she cried.

And he grew, and grew, and grew uneasy . . .

"*Now!*"

He looked down.

He looked down, as the god of our most ancient ancestors might have looked down. Fear, shame, and mocking laughter rang in my head. Her head, too?

"*Now!*"

She looked up at the nascent earthquake.

"I can't!"

It was going to be so damnably simple this time, now the rabbit had died. I reached out.

I stopped.

"Push it yourself."

"I can't. You do it. Land him, Carl!"

"No. If I do, you'll wonder for the rest of your life whether you could have. You'll throw away your soul finding out. I know you will, because we're alike, and I did it that way. Find out now!"

She stared.

I gripped her shoulders.

"Could be that's me out there," I offered. "I am a green sea serpent, a hateful, monstrous beast, and out to destroy you. I am answerable to no one. Push the Inject."

Her hand moved to the button, jerked back.

"Now!"

She pushed it.

I lowered her still form to the floor and finished things up with Ikky.

It was a good seven hours before I awakened to the steady, sea-chewing grind of Tensquare's blades.

"You're sick," commented Mike.

"How's Jean?"

"The same."

"Where's the beast?"

"Here."

"Good." I rolled over. ". . . Didn't get away this time."

So that's the way it was. No one is born a baitman, I don't think, but the rings of Saturn sing epithalamium the sea-beast's dower.

A Rose For Ecclesiastes

I was busy translating one of my *Madrigals Macabre* into Martian on the morning I was found acceptable. The intercom had buzzed briefly, and I dropped my pencil and flipped on the toggle in a single motion.

"Mister G," piped Morton's youthful contralto, "the old man says I should 'get hold of that damned conceited rhymer' right away, and send him to his cabin. Since there's only one damned conceited rhymer . . ."

"Let not ambition mock thy useful toil." I cut him off.

So, the Martians had finally made up their minds! I knocked an inch and a half of ash from a smoldering butt, and took my first drag since I had lit it. The entire month's anticipation tried hard to crowd itself into the moment, but could not quite make it. I was frightened to walk those forty feet and hear Emory say the words I already knew he would say; and that feeling elbowed the other one into the background.

So I finished the stanza I was translating before I got up.

It took only a moment to reach Emory's door. I knocked twice and opened it, just as he growled, "Come in."

"You wanted to see me?" I sat down quickly to save him the trouble of offering me a seat.

"That was fast. What did you do, run?"

I regarded his paternal discontent:

Little fatty flecks beneath pale eyes, thinning hair, and an Irish nose; a voice a decibel louder than anyone else's. . . .

Hamlet to Claudius: "I was working."

"Hah!" he snorted. "Come off it. No one's ever seen you do any of that stuff."

I shrugged my shoulders and started to rise.

"If that's what you called me down here—"

"Sit down!"

He stood up. He walked around his desk. He hovered above me and glared down. (A hard trick, even when I'm in a low chair.)

"You are undoubtedly the most antagonistic bastard I've ever had to work with!" he bellowed, like a belly-stung buffalo. "Why the hell don't you act like a human being sometime and surprise everybody? I'm willing to admit you're smart, maybe even a genius, but—oh, hell!" He made a heaving gesture with both hands and walked back to his chair.

"Betty has finally talked them into letting you go in." His voice was normal again. "They'll receive you this afternoon. Draw one of the jeepsters after lunch, and get down there."

"Okay," I said.

"That's all, then."

I nodded, got to my feet. My hand was on the doorknob when he said:

"I don't have to tell you how important this is. Don't treat them the way you treat us."

I closed the door behind me.

I don't remember what I had for lunch. I was nervous, but I knew instinctively that I wouldn't muff it. My Boston publishers expected a Martian Idyll, or at least a Saint-Exupéry job on space flight. The National Science Association wanted a complete report on the Rise and Fall of the Martian Empire.

They would both be pleased, I knew.

That's the reason everyone is jealous—why they hate me. I always come through, and I can come through better than anyone else.

I shoveled in a final anthill of slop, and made my way to our carbarn. I drew one jeepster and headed it toward Tirellian.

Flames of sand, lousy with iron oxide, set fire to the buggy. They swarmed over the open top and bit through my scarf; they set to work pitting my goggles.

The jeepster, swaying and panting like a little donkey I once rode through the Himalayas, kept kicking me in the seat of the pants. The Mountains of Tirellian shuffled their feet and moved toward me at a cockeyed angle.

Suddenly I was heading uphill, and I shifted gears to accommodate the engine's braying. Not like Gobi, not like the Great Southwestern Desert, I mused. Just red, just dead . . . without even a cactus.

I reached the crest of the hill, but I had raised too much dust to see what was ahead. It didn't matter, though; I have a head full of maps. I bore to the left and downhill, adjusting the throttle. A crosswind and solid ground beat down the fires. I felt like Ulysses in Melebolge—with a terza-rima speech in one hand and an eye out for Dante.

I rounded a rock pagoda and arrived.

Betty waved as I crunched to a halt, then jumped down.

"Hi," I choked, unwinding my scarf and shaking

out a pound and a half of grit. "Like, where do I go and who do I see?"

She permitted herself a brief Germanic giggle—more at my starting a sentence with "like" than at my discomfort—then she started talking. (She is a top linguist, so a word from the Village Idiom still tickles her!)

I appreciate her precise, furry talk; informational, and all that. I had enough in the way of social pleasantries before me to last at least the rest of my life. I looked at her chocolate-bar eyes and perfect teeth, at her sun-bleached hair, close-cropped to the head (I hate blondes!), and decided that she was in love with me.

"Mr. Gallinger, the Matriarch is waiting inside to be introduced. She has consented to open the Temple records for your study." She paused here to pat her hair and squirm a little. Did my gaze make her nervous?

"They are religious documents, as well as their only history," she continued, "sort of like the Mahabharata. She expects you to observe certain rituals in handling them, like repeating the sacred words when you turn pages—she will teach you the system."

I nodded quickly, several times.

"Fine, let's go in."

"Uh—" She paused. "Do not forget their Eleven Forms of Politeness and Degree. They take matters of form quite seriously—and do not get into any discussions over the equality of the sexes—"

"I know all about their taboos," I broke in. "Don't worry. I've lived in the Orient, remember?"

She dropped her eyes and seized my hand. I almost jerked it away.

"It will look better if I enter leading you."

I swallowed my comments, and followed her, like Samson in Gaza.

* * *

Inside, my last thought met with a strange correspondence. The Matriarch's quarters were a rather abstract version of what I imagine the tents of the tribes of Israel to have been like. Abstract, I say, because it was all frescoed brick, peaked like a huge tent, with animal-skin representations like gray-blue scars, that looked as if they had been laid on the walls with a palette knife.

The Matriarch, M'Cwyie, was short, white-haired, fiftyish, and dressed like a Gypsy queen. With her rainbow of voluminous skirts she looked like an inverted punch bowl set atop a cushion.

Accepting my obeisances, she regarded me as an owl might a rabbit. The lids of those black, black eyes jumped upwards as she discovered my perfect accent. The tape recorder Betty had carried on her interviews had done its part, and I knew the language reports from the first two expeditions, verbatim. I'm all hell when it comes to picking up accents.

"You are the poet?"

"Yes," I replied.

"Recite one of your poems, please."

"I'm sorry, but nothing short of a thorough translating job would do justice to your language and my poetry, and I don't know enough of your language yet."

"Oh?"

"But I've been making such translations for my own amusement, as an exercise in grammar," I continued. "I'd be honored to bring a few of them along one of the times that I come here."

"Yes. Do so."

Score one for me!

She turned to Betty.

"You may go now."

Betty muttered the parting formalities, gave me a strange sidewise look, and was gone. She apparently had expected to stay and "assist" me. She wanted a piece of the glory, like everyone else. But I was the Schliemann at this Troy, and there would be only one name on the Association report!

M'Cwyie rose, and I noticed that she gained very little height by standing. But then I'm six-six and look like a poplar in October: thin, bright red on top, and towering above everyone else.

"Our records are very, very old," she began. "Betty says that your word for their age is 'millennia.'"

I nodded appreciatively.

"I'm very eager to see them."

"They are not here. We will have to go into the Temple—they may not be removed."

I was suddenly wary.

"You have no objections to my copying them, do you?"

"No. I see that you respect them, or your desire would not be so great."

"Excellent."

She seemed amused. I asked her what was funny.

"The High Tongue may not be so easy for a foreigner to learn."

It came through fast.

No one on the first expedition had gotten this close. I had had no way of knowing that this was a double-language deal—a classical as well as a vulgar. I knew some of their Prakrit, now I had to learn all their Sanskrit.

"Ouch! and damn!"

"Pardon, please?"

"It's non-translatable, M'Cwyie. But imagine yourself having to learn the High Tongue in a hurry, and you can guess at the sentiment."

She seemed amused again, and told me to remove my shoes.

She guided me through an alcove . . .

. . . and into a burst of Byzantine brilliance!

* * *

No Earthman had ever been in this room before, or I would have heard about it. Carter, the first expedition's linguist, with the help of one Mary Allen, M.D., had learned all the grammar and vocabulary that I knew while sitting cross-legged in the antechamber.

We had had no idea this existed. Greedily, I cast my eyes about. A highly sophisticated system of esthetics lay behind the decor. We would have to revise our entire estimation of Martian culture.

For one thing, the ceiling was vaulted and corbeled; for another, there were side-columns with reverse flutings; for another—oh hell! The place was big. Posh. You could never have guessed it from the shaggy outsides.

I bent forward to study the gilt filigree on a ceremonial table. M'Cwyie seemed a bit smug at my intentness, but I'd still have hated to play poker with her.

The table was loaded with books.

With my toe, I traced a mosaic on the floor.

"Is your entire city within this one building?"

"Yes, it goes far back into the mountain."

"I see," I said, seeing nothing.

I couldn't ask her for a conducted tour, yet.

She moved to a small stool by the table.

"Shall we begin your friendship with the High Tongue?"

I was trying to photograph the hall with my eyes, knowing I would have to get a camera in here, somehow, sooner or later. I tore my gaze from a statuette and nodded, hard.

"Yes, introduce me."

I sat down.

For the next three weeks alphabet-bugs chased each other behind my eyelids whenever I tried to sleep. The sky was an unclouded pool of turquoise that rippled calligraphies whenever I swept my eyes across it. I drank quarts of coffee while I worked and mixed cocktails of Benzedrine and champagne for my coffee breaks.

M'Cwyie tutored me two hours every morning, and occasionally for another two in the evening. I spent an additional fourteen hours a day on my own, once I had gotten up sufficient momentum to go ahead alone.

And at night the elevator of time dropped me to its bottom floors. . . .

I was six again, learning my Hebrew, Greek, Latin, and Aramaic. I was ten, sneaking peeks at the *Iliad*. When Daddy wasn't spreading hellfire brimstone, and brotherly love, he was teaching me to dig the Word, like in the original.

Lord! There are so many originals and so *many* words! When I was twelve I started pointing out the little differences between what he was preaching and what I was reading.

The fundamentalist vigor of his reply brooked no debate. It was worse than any beating. I kept my mouth shut after that and learned to appreciate Old Testament poetry.

—Lord, I am sorry! Daddy—Sir—I am sorry! —It couldn't be! It couldn't be . . .

On the day the boy graduated from high school, with French, German, Spanish, and Latin awards, Dad Gallinger had told his fourteen-year-old, six-foot scarecrow of a son that he wanted him to enter the ministry. I remember how his son was evasive:

"Sir," he had said, "I'd sort of like to study on my own for a year or so, and then take pre-theology courses at some liberal arts university. I feel I'm still sort of young to try a seminary, straight off."

The Voice of God: "But you have the gift of tongues, my son. You can preach the Gospel in all the lands of Babel. You were born to be a missionary. You say you are young, but time is rushing by you like a whirlwind. Start early, and you will enjoy added years of service."

The added years of service were so many added tails to the cat repeatedly laid on my back. I can't see his face now; I never can. Maybe it is because I was always afraid to look at it then.

And years later, when he was dead, and laid out, in black, amidst bouquets, amidst weeping congregationalists, amidst prayers, red faces, handkerchiefs, hands patting your shoulders, solemn faced comforters . . . I looked at him and did not recognize him.

We had met nine months before my birth, this stranger and I. He had never been cruel—stern, demanding, with contempt for everyone's shortcomings —but never cruel. He was also all that I had had of a mother. And brothers. And sisters. He had tolerated my three years at St. John's, possibly because of its name, never knowing how liberal and delightful a place it really was.

But I never knew him, and the man atop the catafalque demanded nothing now; I was free not to preach the Word. But now I wanted to, in a different way. I wanted to preach a word that I could never have voiced while he lived.

I did not return for my senior year in the fall. I had a small inheritance coming, and a bit of trouble getting control of it, since I was still under eighteen. But I managed.

It was Greenwich Village I finally settled upon.

Not telling any well-meaning parishioners my new address, I entered into a daily routine of writing poetry and teaching myself Japanese and Hindustani. I grew a fiery beard, drank espresso, and learned to play chess. I wanted to try a couple of the other paths to salvation.

After that, it was two years in India with the Old Peace Corps—which broke me of my Buddhism, and gave me my *Pipes of Krishna* lyrics and the Pulitzer they deserved.

Then back to the States for my degree, grad work in linguistics, and more prizes.

Then one day a ship went to Mars. The vessel settling in its New Mexico nest of fires contained a new language. It was fantastic, exotic, and esthetically overpowering. After I had learned all there was to know about it, and written my book, I was famous in new circles:

"Go, Gallinger. Dip your bucket in the well, and bring us a drink of Mars. Go, learn another world—but remain aloof, rail at it gently like Auden—and hand us its soul in iambics."

And I came to the land where the sun is a tarnished penny, where the wind is a whip, where two moons play at hot rod games, and a hell of sand gives you the incendiary itches whenever you look at it.

I rose from my twistings on the bunk and crossed the darkened cabin to a port. The desert was a carpet of endless orange, bulging from the sweepings of centuries beneath it.

"I a stranger, unafraid —This is the land —I've got it made!"

I laughed.

I had the High Tongue by the tail already—or the roots, if you want your puns anatomical, as well as correct.

The High and Low Tongues were not so dissimilar as they had first seemed. I had enough of the one to get me through the murkier parts of the other. I had the grammar and all the commoner irregular verbs down cold; the dictionary I was constructing grew by the day, like a tulip, and would bloom shortly. Every time I played the tapes the stem lengthened.

Now was the time to tax my ingenuity, to really drive the lessons home. I had purposely refrained from plunging into the major texts until I could do justice to them. I had been reading minor commentaries, bits of verse, fragments of history. And one thing had impressed me strongly in all that I read.

They wrote about concrete things: rock, sand, water, winds; and the tenor couched within these elemental symbols was fiercely pessimistic. It reminded me of some Buddhist texts, but even more so, I realized from my recent *recherches*, it was like parts of the Old Testament. Specifically, it reminded me of the Book of Ecclesiastes.

That, then, would be it. The sentiment, as well as the vocabulary, was so similar that it would be a perfect exercise. Like putting Poe into French. I would never be a convert to the Way of Malann, but I would show them that an Earthman had once thought the same thoughts, felt similarly.

I switched on my desk lamp and sought King James amidst my books.

Vanity of vanities, saith the Preacher, vanity of vanities; all is vanity. What profit hath a man . . .

My progress seemed to startle M'Cwyie. She peered at me, like Sartre's Other, across the tabletop. I ran through a chapter in the Book of Locar. I didn't look up, but I could feel the tight net her eyes were working about my head, shoulders, and rapid hands. I turned another page.

Was she weighing the net, judging the size of the catch? And what for? The books said nothing of fishers on Mars. Especially of men. They said that some god named Malann had spat, or had done something disgusting (depending on the version you read), and that life had gotten underway as a disease in inorganic matter. They said that movement was its first law, its first law, and that the dance was the only legitimate reply to the inorganic . . . the dance's quality its justification, —fication . . . and love is a disease in organic matter— Inorganic matter?

I shook my head. I had almost been asleep.

"M'narra."

I stood and stretched. Her eyes outlined me greedily now. So I met them, and they dropped.

"I grow tired. I want to rest awhile. I didn't sleep much last night."

She nodded, Earth's shorthand for "yes," as she had learned from me.

"You wish to relax, and see the explicitness of the doctrine of Locar in its fullness?"

"Pardon me?"

"You wish to see a Dance of Locar?"

"Oh." Their damned circuits of form and periphrasis here ran worse than the Korean! "Yes. Surely. Any time it's going to be done I'd be happy to watch."

I continued, "In the meantime, I've been meaning to ask you whether I might take some pictures—"

"Now is the time. Sit down. Rest. I will call the muscians."

She bustled out through a door I had never been past.

Well now, the dance was the highest art, according to Locar, not to mention Havelock Ellis, and I was about to see how their centuries-dead philosopher felt it should be conducted. I rubbed my eyes and snapped over, touching my toes a few times.

The blood began pounding in my head, and I sucked in a couple deep breaths. I bent again and there was a flurry of motion at the door.

To the trio who entered with M'Cwyie I must have looked as if I were searching for the marbles I had just lost, bent over like that.

I grinned weakly and straightened up, my face red from more than exertion. I hadn't expected them *that* quickly.

Suddenly I thought of Havelock Ellis again in his area of greatest popularity.

The little redheaded doll, wearing, sari-like, a diaphanous piece of the Martian sky, looked up in wonder—as a child at some colorful flag on a high pole.

"Hello," I said, or its equivalent.

She bowed before replying. Evidently I had been promoted in status.

"I shall dance," said the red wound in that pale, pale cameo, her face. Eyes, the color of dream and her dress, pulled away from mine.

She drifted to the center of the room.

Standing there, like a figure in an Etruscan frieze, she was either meditating or regarding the design on the floor.

Was the mosaic symbolic of something? I studied it. If it was, it eluded me; it would make an attractive bathroom floor or patio, but I couldn't see much in it beyond that.

The other two were paint-spattered sparrows like M'Cwyie, in their middle years. One settled to the floor with a triple-stringed instrument faintly resembling a *samisen*. The other held a simple woodblock and two drumsticks.

M'Cwyie disdained her stool and was seated upon the floor before I realized it. I followed suit.

The *samisen* player was still tuning it up, so I leaned toward M'Cwyie.

"What is the dancer's name?"

"Braxa," she replied, without looking at me, and raised her left hand, slowly, which meant yes, and go ahead, and let it begin.

The stringed-thing throbbed like a toothache, and a ticktocking, like ghosts of all the clocks they had never invented, sprang from the block.

Braxa was a statue, both hands raised to her face, elbows high and outspread.

The music became a metaphor for fire.

Crackle, purr, snap . . .

She did not move.

The hissing altered to splashes. The cadence slowed.

It was water now, the most precious thing in the world, gurgling clear and green over mossy rocks.

Still she did not move.

Glissandos. A pause.

Then, so faint I could hardly be sure at first, the tremble of the winds began. Softly, gently, sighing and halting, uncertain. A pause, a sob, then a repetition of the first statement, only louder.

Were my eyes completely bugged from my reading, or was Braxa actually trembling all over, head to foot?

She was.

She began a microscopic swaying. A fraction of an inch right, then left. Her fingers opened like the petals of a flower, and I could see that her eyes were closed.

Her eyes opened. They were distant, glassy, looking through me and the walls. Her swaying became more pronounced, merged with the beat.

The wind was sweeping in from the desert now, falling against Tirellian like waves on a dike. Her fingers moved, they were the gusts. Her arms, slow pendulums, descended, began a counter-movement.

The gale was coming now. She began an axial movement and her hands caught up with the rest of her body, only now her shoulders commenced to writhe out a figure-eight.

The wind! The wind, I say. O wild, enigmatic! O muse of St. John Perse!

The cyclone was twisting around those eyes, its still center. Her head was thrown back, but I knew there was no ceiling between her gaze, passive as Buddha's, and the unchanging skies. Only the two moons, perhaps, interrupted their slumber in that elemental Nirvana of uninhabited turquoise.

Years ago, I had seen the Devadais in India, the street-dancers, spinning their colorful webs, drawing in the male insect. But Braxa was more than this: she was a Ramadjany, like those votaries of Rama, incarnation of Vishnu, who had given the dance to man: the sacred dancers.

The clicking was monotonously steady now; the whine of the strings made me think of the stinging rays of the sun, their heat stolen by the wind's halations; the blue was Sarasvati and Mary, and a girl named Laura. I heard a sitar from somewhere, watched this statue come to life, and inhaled a divine afflatus.

I was again Rimbaud with his hashish, Baudelaire with his laudanum, Poe, De Quincy, Wilde, Mallarme and Aleister Crowley. I was, for a fleeting second, my father in his dark pulpit and darker suit, the hymns and the organ's wheeze transmuted to bright wind.

She was a spun weather vane, a feathered crucifix hovering in the air, a clothesline holding one bright garment lashed parallel to the ground. Her shoulder was bare now, and her right breast moved up and down like a moon in the sky, its red nipple appearing momentarily above a fold and vanishing again. The music was as formal as Job's argument with God. Her dance was God's reply.

The music slowed, settled; it had been met, matched, answered. Her garment, as if alive, crept back into the more sedate folds it originally held.

She dropped low, lower, to the floor. Her head fell upon her raised knees. She did not move.

There was silence.

I realized, from the ache across my shoulders, how tensely I had been sitting. My armpits were wet.

Rivulets had been running down my sides. What did one do now? Applaud?

I sought M'Cwyie from the corner of my eye. She raised her right hand.

As if by telepathy the girl shuddered all over and stood. The musicians also rose. So did M'Cwyie.

I got to my feet, with a charley horse in my left leg, and said, "It was beautiful," inane as that sounds.

I received three different High Forms of "thank you."

There was a flurry of color and I was alone again with M'Cwyie.

"That is the 117th of the 2,224 dances of Locar."

I looked down at her.

"Whether Locar was right or wrong, he worked a fine reply to the inorganic."

She smiled.

"Are the dances of your world like this?"

"Some of them are similar. I was reminded of them as I watched Braxa—but I've never seen anything exactly like hers."

"She is very good," M'Cwyie said. "She knows all the dances."

A hint of her earlier expression which had troubled me . . .

It was gone in an instant.

"I must tend my duties now." She moved to the table and closed the books. "M'narra."

"Good-bye." I slipped into my boots.

"Good-bye, Gallinger."

I walked out the door, mounted the jeepster, and roared across the evening into night, my wings of risen desert flapping slowly behind me.

II

I had just closed the door behind Betty, after a brief grammar session, when I heard the voices in the hall. My vent was opened a fraction, so I stood there and eavesdropped:

Morton's fruity treble: "Guess what? He said 'hello' to me awhile ago."

"Hmmph!" Emory's elephant lungs exploded. "Either he's slipping, or you were standing in his way and he wanted you to move."

"Probably didn't recognize me. I don't think he sleeps any more, now he has that language to play with. I had night watch last week, and every night I passed his door at 0300—I always heard that recorder going. At 0500 when I got off, he was still at it."

"The guy *is* working hard," Emory admitted, grudgingly. "In fact, I think he's taking some kind of dope to keep awake. He looks sort of glassy-eyed these days. Maybe that's natural for a poet, though."

Betty had been standing there, because she broke in then:

"Regardless of what you think of him, it's going to take me at least a year to learn what he's picked up in three weeks. And I'm just a linguist, not a poet."

Morton must have been nursing a crush on her bovine charms. It's the only reason I can think of for his dropping his guns to say what he did.

"I took a course in modern poetry when I was back at the university," he began. "We read six authors—Yeats, Pound, Eliot, Crane, Stevens, and Gallinger—and on the last day of the semester, when the prof was feeling a little rhetorical, he said, 'These six names are written on the century, and all the gates of criticism and hell shall not prevail against them.'

"Myself," he continued, "I thought his *Pipes of Krishna* and his *Madrigals* were great. I was honored to be chosen for an expedition he was going on.

I think he's spoken two dozen words to me since I met him," he finished.

The Defense: "Did it ever occur to you," Betty said, "that he might be tremendously self-conscious about his appearance? He was also a precocious child, and probably never even had school friends. He's sensitive and very introverted."

"Sensitive? Self-conscious?" Emory choked and gagged. "The man is as proud as Lucifer, and he's a walking insult machine. You press a button like 'Hello' or 'Nice day' and he thumbs his nose at you. He's got it down to a reflex."

They muttered a few other pleasantries and drifted away.

Well bless you, Morton boy. You little pimple-faced, Ivy-bred connoisseur! I've never taken a course in my poetry, but I'm glad someone said that. The Gates of Hell. Well now! Maybe Daddy's prayers got heard somewhere, and I am a missionary, after all!

Only . . .

. . . Only a missionary needs something to convert people *to*. I have my private system of esthetics, and I suppose it oozes an ethical by-product somewhere. But if I ever had anything to preach, really, even in my poems, I wouldn't care to preach it to such lowlifes as you. If you think I'm a slob, I'm also a snob, and there's no room for you in my Heaven— it's a private place, where Swift, Shaw, and Petronius Arbiter came to dinner.

And oh, the feasts we have! The Trimalchio's, the Emory's we dissect!

We finish you with the soup, Morton!

I turned and settled at my desk. I wanted to write something. Ecclesiastes could take a night off. I wanted to write a poem, a poem about the 117th dance of Locar; about a rose following the light, traced by the wind, sick, like Blake's rose, dying. . . .

I found a pencil and began.

When I had finished, I was pleased. It wasn't great—at least, it was no greater than it needed to be—High Martian not being my strongest tongue. I groped and put it into English, with partial rhymes. Maybe I'd stick it in my next book. I called it *Braxa:*

In a land of wind and red, where the icy evening of Time freezes milk in the breasts of Life, as two moons overhead—cat and dog in alleyways of dream— scratch and scramble agelessly my flight . . .

This final flower turns a burning head.

I put it away and found some phenobarbital. I was suddenly tired.

When I showed my poem to M'Cwyie the next day, she read it through several times, very slowly.

"It is lovely," she said. "But you used three words from your own language. 'Cat' and 'dog,' I assume, are two small animals with a hereditary hatred for one another. But what is 'flower?'"

"Oh," I said. "I've never come across your word for 'flower,' but I was actually thinking of an Earth flower, the rose."

"What is it like?"

"Well, its petals are generally bright red. That's what I meant, on one level, by 'burning heads.' I also wanted it to imply fever, though, and red hair, and the fire of life. The rose, itself, has a thorny stem, green leaves, and a distinct, pleasing aroma."

"I wish I could see one."

"I suppose it could be arranged. I'll check."

"Do it, please. You are a—" She used the word for "prophet," or religious poet, like Isais or Locar. "—and your poem is inspired. I shall tell Braxa of it."

I declined the nomination, but felt flattered.

This, then, I decided, was the strategic day, the day on which to ask whether I might bring in the microfilm machine and the camera. I wanted to copy all their texts, I explained, and I couldn't write fast enough to do it.

She surprised me by agreeing immediately. But she bowled me over with her invitation.

"Would you like to come and stay here while you do this thing? Then you can work night and day, any time you want—except when the Temple is being used, of course."

I bowed.

"I should be honored."

"Good. Bring your machines when you want, and I will show you a room."

"Will this afternoon be all right?"

"Certainly."

"Then I will go now and get things ready. Until this afternoon . . ."

"Good-bye."

I anticipated a little trouble from Emory, but not much. Everyone back at the ship was anxious to see the Martians, poke needles in the Martians, ask them about Martian climate, diseases, soil chemistry, politics, and mushrooms (our botanist was a fungus nut, but a reasonably good guy)—and only four or five had actually gotten to see them. The crew had been spending most of its time excavating dead cities and their acropolises. We played the game by strict rules, and the natives were as fiercely insular as the nineteenth-century Japanese. I figured I would meet with little resistance, and I figured right.

In fact, I got the distinct impression that everyone was happy to see me move out.

I stopped in the hydroponics room to speak with our mushroom master.

"Hi, Kane. Grow any toadstools in the sand yet?"

He sniffed. He always sniffs. Maybe he's allergic to plants.

"Hello, Gallinger. No, I haven't had any success with toadstools, but look behind the carbarn next time you're out there. I've got a few cacti going."

"Great," I observed. Doc Kane was about my only friend aboard, not counting Betty.

"Say, I came down to ask you a favor."

"Name it."

"I want a rose."

"A what?"

"A rose. You know, a nice red American Beauty job—thorns, pretty smelling—"

"I don't think it will take in this soil. *Sniff, sniff.*"

"No, you don't understand. I don't want to plant it, I just want the flowers."

"I'd have to use the tanks." He scratched his hairless dome. "It would take at least three months to get you flowers, even under forced growth."

"Will you do it?"

"Sure, if you don't mind the wait."

"Not at all. In fact, three months will just make it before we leave." I looked about at the pools of crawling slime, at the trays of shoots. "I'm moving up to Tirellian today, but I'll be in and out all the time. I'll be here when it blooms."

"Moving up there, eh? Moore said they're an in-group."

"I guess I'm 'in' then."

"Looks that way—I still don't see how you learned their language, though. Of course, I had trouble with French and German for my Ph.D, but last week I heard Betty demonstrate it at lunch. It just sounds like a lot of weird noises. She says speaking it is like working a *Times* crossword and trying to imitate birdcalls at the same time."

I laughed, and took the cigarette he offered me.

"It's complicated," I acknowledged. "But, well, it's as if you suddenly came across a whole new class of mycetae here—you'd dream about it at night."

His eyes were gleaming.

"Wouldn't that be something! I might, yet, you know."

"Maybe you will."

He chuckled as we walked to the door.

"I'll start your roses tonight. Take it easy down there."

"You bet. Thanks."

Like I said, a fungus nut, but a fairly good guy.

My quarters in the Citadel of Tirellian were directly adjacent to the Temple, on the inward side and slightly to the left. They were a considerable improvement over my cramped cabin, and I was pleased that Martian culture had progressed sufficiently to discover the desirability of the mattress over the pallet. Also, the bed was long enough to accommodate me, which was surprising.

So I unpacked and took sixteen 35 mm. shots of the Temple, before starting on the books.

I took 'stats until I was sick of turning pages without knowing what they said. So I started translating a work of history.

"Lo. In the thirty-seventh year of the Process of Cillen the rains came, which gave rise to rejoicing, for it was a rare and untoward occurrence, and commonly construed a blessing.

"But it was not the life-giving semen of Malann which fell from the heavens. It was the blood of the universe, spurting from an artery. And the last days were upon us. The final dance was to begin.

"The rains brought the plague that does not kill, and the last passes of Locar began with their drumming. . . ."

I asked myself what the hell Tamur meant, for he was an historian and supposedly committed to fact. This was not their Apocalypse.

Unless they could be one and the same . . . ?

Why not? I mused. Tirellian's handful of people were the remnant of what had obviously once been a highly developed culture. They had had wars, but no holocausts; science, but little technology. A plague, a plague that did not kill . . . ? Could that have done it? How, if it wasn't fatal?

I read on, but the nature of the plague was not discussed. I turned pages, skipped ahead, and drew a blank.

M'Cwyie! M'Cwyie! When I want to question you most, you are not around!

Would it be a *faux pas* to go looking for her? Yes, I decided. I was restricted to the rooms I had been shown, that had been an implicit understanding. I would have to wait to find out.

So I cursed long and loud, in many languages, doubtless burning Malann's sacred ears, there in his Temple.

He did not see fit to strike me dead, so I decided to call it a day and hit the sack.

I must have been asleep for several hours when Braxa entered my room with a tiny lamp. She dragged me awake by tugging at my pajama sleeve.

I said hello. Thinking back, there is not much else I could have said.

"Hello."

"I have come," she said, "to hear the poem."

'What poem?"

"Yours."

"Oh."

I yawned, sat up, and did things people usually do when awakened in the middle of the night to read poetry.

"That is very kind of you, but isn't the hour a trifle awkward?"

"I don't mind," she said.

Someday I am going to write an article for the

Journal of Semantics, called "Tone of Voice: An Insufficient Vehicle for Irony."

However, I was awake, so I grabbed my robe.

"What sort of animal is that?" she asked, pointing at the silk dragon on my lapel.

"Mythical," I replied. "Now look, it's late. I am tired. I have much to do in the morning. And M'Cwyie just might get the wrong idea if she learns you were here."

"Wrong idea?"

"You know damned well what I mean!" It was the first time I had had an opportunity to use Martian profanity, and it failed.

"No," she said, "I do not know."

She seemed frightened, like a puppy being scolded without knowing what it has done wrong.

I softened. Her red cloak matched her hair and lips so perfectly, and those lips were trembling.

"Here now, I didn't mean to upset you. On my world there are certain, uh, mores, concerning people of different sex alone together in bedrooms, and not allied by marriage. . . . Um, I mean, you see what I mean?"

"No."

They were jade, her eyes.

"Well, it's sort of . . . Well, it's sex, that's what it is."

A light switched on in those jade lamps.

"Oh, you mean having children!"

"Yes. That's it! Exactly."

She laughed. It was the first time I had heard laughter in Tirellian. It sounded like a violinist striking his high strings with the bow, in short little chops. It was not an altogether pleasant thing to hear, especially because she laughed too long.

When she had finished she moved closer.

"I remember, now," she said. "We used to have such rules. Half a Process ago, when I was a child, we had such rules. But"—she looked as if she were ready to laugh again—"there is no need for them now."

My mind moved like a tape recorder played at triple speed.

Half a Process! HalfaProcessa-ProcessaProcess! No! Yes! Half a Process was 243 years, roughly speaking!

—Time enough to learn the 2224 dances of Locar.
—Time enough to grow old, if you were human.
—Earth-style human, I mean.

I looked at her again, pale as the white queen in an ivory chess set.

She was human, I'd stake my soul—alive, normal, healthy. I'd stake my life—woman, my body . . .

But she was two and a half centuries old, which made M'Cwyie Methuselah's grandma. It flattered me to think of their repeated complimenting of my skills, as linguist, as poet. These superior beings!

But what did she mean "there is no such need for them now"? Why the near-hysteria? Why all those funny looks I'd been getting from M'Cwyie?

I suddenly knew I was close to something important, besides a beautiful girl.

"Tell me," I said, in my Casual Voice, "did it have anything to do with 'the plague that does not kill,' of which Tamur wrote?"

"Yes," she replied, "the children born after the Rains could have no children of their own, and—"

"And what?" I was leaning forward, memory set at "record."

"—and the men had no desire to get any."

I sagged backward against the bedpost. Racial sterility, masculine impotence, following phenomenal weather. Had some vagabond cloud of radioactive junk from God knows where penetrated their weak atmosphere one day? One day long before Shiaparelli saw the canals, mythical as my dragon, before those "canals" had given rise to some correct guesses for all the wrong reasons, had Braxa been alive, dancing, here—damned in the womb since blind Milton had written of another paradise, equally lost?

I found a cigarette. Good thing I had thought to bring ashtrays. Mars had never had a tobacco industry either. Or booze. The ascetics I had met in India had been Dionysiac compared to this.

"What is that tube of fire?"

"A cigarette. Want one?"

"Yes, please."

She sat beside me, and I lighted it for her.

"It irritates the nose."

"Yes. Draw some into your lungs, hold it there, and exhale."

A moment paused.

"Ooh," she said.

A pause, then, "Is it sacred?"

"No, it's nicotine," I answered, "a very *ersatz* form of divinity."

Another pause.

"Please don't ask me to translate 'ersatz.' "

"I won't. I get this feeling sometimes when I dance."

"It will pass in a moment."

"Tell me your poem now."

An idea hit me.

"Wait a minute," I said; "I may have something better."

I got up and rummaged through my notebooks, then I returned and sat beside her.

"These are the first three chapters of the Book of Ecclesiastes," I explained. "It is very similar to your own sacred books."

I started reading.

I got through eleven verses before she cried out, "Please don't read that! Tell me one of yours!"

I stopped and tossed the notebook onto a nearby table. She was shaking, not as she had quivered that day she danced as the wind, but with the jitter of unshed tears. She held her cigarette awkwardly, like a pencil. Clumsily, I put my arm about her shoulders.

"He is so sad," she said, "like all the others."

So I twisted my mind like a bright ribbon, folded it, and tied the crazy Christmas knots I love so well. From German to Martian, with love, I did an impromptu paraphrasal of a poem about a Spanish dancer. I thought it would please her. I was right.

"Ooh," she said again. "Did you write that?"

"No, it's by a better man than I."

"I don't believe you. You wrote it."

"No, a man named Rilke did."

"But you brought it across to my language. Light another match, so I can see how she danced."

I did.

"The fires of forever," she mused, "and she stamped them out, 'with small, firm feet.' I wish I could dance like that."

"You're better than any Gypsy," I laughed, blowing it out.

"No, I'm not. I couldn't do that. Do you want me to dance for you?"

Her cigarette was burning down, so I removed it from her fingers and put it out, along with my own.

"No," I said. "Go to bed."

She smiled, and before I realized it, had unclasped the fold of red at her shoulder.

And everything fell away.

And I swallowed, with some difficulty.

"All right," she said.

So I kissed her, as the breath of fallen cloth extinguished the lamp.

III

The days were like Shelley's leaves: yellow, red, brown, whipped in bright gusts by the west wind.

They swirled past me with the rattle of microfilm. Almost all the books were recorded now. It would take scholars years to get through them, to properly assess their value. Mars was locked in my desk.

Ecclesiastes, abandoned and returned to a dozen times, was almost ready to speak in the High Tongue.

I whistled when I wasn't in the Temple. I wrote reams of poetry I would have been ashamed of before. Evenings I would walk with Braxa, across the dunes or up into the mountains. Sometimes she would dance for me; and I would read something long, and in dactylic hexameter. She still thought I was Rilke, and I almost kidded myself into believing it. Here I was, staying at the Castle Duino, writing his *Elegies*.

*. . . It is strange to inhabit the Earth no more,
to use no longer customs scarce acquired,
nor interpret roses . . .*

No! Never interpret roses! Don't. Smell them (sniff, Kane!), pick them, enjoy them. Live in the moment. Hold to it tightly. But charge not the gods to explain. So fast the leaves go by, are blown . . .

And no one ever noticed us. Or cared.

Laura. Laura and Braxa. They rhyme, you know, with a bit of a clash. Tall, cool, and blonde was she (I hate blondes!), and Daddy had turned me inside out, like a pocket, and I thought she could fill me again. But the big, beat word-slinger, with Judas-beard and dog-trust in his eyes, oh, he had been a fine decoration at her parties. And that was all.

How the machine cursed me in the Temple! It blasphemed Malann and Gallinger. And the wild west wind went by and something was not far behind.

The last days were upon us.

A day went by and I did not see Braxa, and a night.

And a second. A third.

I was half-mad. I hadn't realized how close we had become, how important she had been. With the dumb assurance of presence, I had fought against questioning roses.

I had to ask. I didn't want to, but I had no choice.

"Where is she, M'Cwyie? Where is Braxa?"

"She is gone," she said.

"Where?"

"I do not know."

I looked at those devil-bird eyes. Anathema maranatha rose to my lips.

"I must know."

She looked through me.

"She has left us. She is gone. Up into the hills, I suppose. Or the desert. It does not matter. What does anything matter? The dance draws to a close. The Temple will soon be empty."

"Why? Why did she leave?"

"I do not know."

"I must see her again. We lift off in a matter of days."

"I am sorry, Gallinger."

"So am I," I said, and slammed shut a book without saying "m'narra."

I stood up.

"I will find her."

I left the Temple. M'Cwyie was a seated statue. My boots were still where I had left them.

All day I roared up and down the dunes, going nowhere. To the crew of the *Aspic* I must have looked like a sandstorm, all by myself. Finally, I had to return for more fuel.

Emory came stalking out.

"Okay, made it good. You look like the abominable dust man. Why the rodeo?"

"Why, I, uh, lost something."

"In the middle of the desert? Was it one of your sonnets? They're the only thing I can think of that you'd make such a fuss over."

"No, dammit! It was something personal."

George had finished filling the tank. I started to mount the jeepster again.

"Hold on there!" he grabbed my arm.

"You're not going back until you tell me what this is all about."

I could have broken his grip, but then he could order me dragged back by the heels, and quite a few people would enjoy doing the dragging. So I forced myself to speak slowly, softly:

"It's simply that I lost my watch. My mother gave it to me and it's a family heirloom. I want to find it before we leave."

"You sure it's not in your cabin, or down in Tirellian?"

"I've already checked."

"Maybe somebody hid it to irritate you. You know you're not the most popular guy around."

I shook my head.

"I thought of that. But I always carry it in my right pocket. I think it might have bounced out going over the dunes."

He narrowed his eyes.

"I remember reading on a book jacket that your mother died when you were born."

"That's right," I said, biting my tongue. "The watch belonged to her father and she wanted me to have it. My father kept it for me."

"Hmph!" he snorted. "That's a pretty strange way to look for a watch, riding up and down in a jeepster."

"I could see the light shining off it that way," I offered, lamely.

"Well, it's starting to get dark," he observed. "No sense looking any more today."

"Throw a dust sheet over the jeepster," he directed a mechanic.

He patted my arm.

"Come on in and get a shower, and something to eat. You look as if you could use both."

Little fatty flecks beneath pale eyes, thinning hair, and an Irish nose; a voice a decibel louder than anyone else's. . . .

His only qualification for leadership!

I stood there, hating him. Claudius! If only this were the fifth act!

But suddenly the idea of a shower, and food, came through to me. I could use both badly. If I insisted on hurrying back immediately I might arouse more suspicion.

So I brushed some sand from my sleeve.

"You're right. That sounds like a good idea."

"Come on, we'll eat in my cabin."

The shower was a blessing, clean khakis were the grace of God, and the food smelled like Heaven.

"Smells pretty good," I said.

We hacked up our steaks in silence. When we got to the dessert and coffee he suggested:

"Why don't you take the night off? Stay here and get some sleep."

I shook my head.

"I'm pretty busy. Finishing up. There's not much time left."

"A couple of days ago you said you were almost finished."

"Almost, but not quite."

"You also said they'll be holding a service in the Temple tonight."

"That's right. I'm going to work in my room."

He shrugged his shoulders.

Finally, he said, "Gallinger," and I looked up because my name means trouble.

"It shouldn't be any of my business," he said, "but it is. Betty says you have a girl down there."

There was no question mark. It was a statement hanging in the air. Waiting.

Betty, you're a bitch. You're a cow and a bitch. And a jealous one, at that. Why didn't you keep your nose where it belonged, shut your eyes? Your mouth?

"So?" I said, a statement with a question mark.

"So," he answered it, "it is my duty, as head of this expedition, to see that relations with the natives are carried on in a friendly, and diplomatic manner."

"You speak of them," I said, "as though they are aborigines. Nothing could be further from the truth."

I rose.

"When my papers are published everyone on Earth will know that's true. I'll tell them things Doctor. Moore never even guessed at. I'll tell the tragedy of a doomed race, waiting for death, resigned and disinterested. I'll tell why, and it will break hard, scholarly hearts. I'll write about it, and they will give me more prizes, and this time I won't want them.

"My God!" I exclaimed. "They had a culture when our ancestors were clubbing the saber-tooth and finding out how fire works!"

"*Do* you have a girl down there?"

"Yes!" I said. Yes, *Claudius! Yes, Daddy! Yes, Emory!* "I do. But I'm going to let you in on a scholarly scoop now. They're already dead. They're sterile. In one more generation there won't be any Martians."

I paused, then added, "Except in my papers, except on a few pieces of microfilm and tape. And in some poems, about a girl who did give a damn and could only bitch about the unfairness of it all by dancing."

"Oh," he said.

After awhile:

"You *have* been behaving differently these past

couple months. You've even been downright civil on occasion, you know. I couldn't help wondering what was happening. I didn't know anything mattered that strongly to you."

I bowed my head.

"Is she the reason you were racing around the desert?"

I nodded.

"Why?"

I looked up.

"Because she's out there, somewhere. I don't know where, or why. And I've got to find her before we go."

"Oh," he said again.

Then he leaned back, opened a drawer, and took out something wrapped in a towel. He unwound it. A framed photo of a woman lay on the table.

"My wife," he said.

It was an attractive face, with big, almond eyes.

"I'm a Navy man, you know," he began. "Young officer once. Met her in Japan."

"Where I come from it wasn't considered right to marry into another race, so we never did. But she was my wife. When she died I was on the other side of the world. They took my children, and I've never seen them since. I couldn't learn what orphanage, what home they were put into. That was long ago. Very few people know about it."

"I'm sorry," I said.

"Don't be. Forget it. But"—he shifted in his chair and looked at me—"if you do want to take her back with you—do it. It'll mean my neck, but I'm too old to ever head another expedition like this one. So go ahead."

He gulped his cold coffee.

"Get your jeepster."

He swiveled the chair around.

I tried to say "thank you" twice, but I couldn't. So I got up and walked out.

"Sayonara, and all that," he muttered behind me.

"Here it is, Gallinger!" I heard a shout.

I turned on my heel and looked back up the ramp.

"Kane!"

He was limned in the port, shadow against light, but I had heard him sniff.

I returned the few steps.

"Here what is?"

"Your rose."

He produced a plastic container, divided internally. The lower half was filled with liquid. The stem ran down into it. The other half, a glass of claret in this horrible night, was a large, newly opened rose.

"Thank you," I said, tucking it into my jacket.

"Going back to Tirellian, eh?"

"Yes."

"I saw you come aboard, so I got it ready. Just missed you at the Captain's cabin. He was busy. Hollered out that I could catch you at the barns."

"Thanks again."

"It's chemically treated. It will stay in bloom for weeks."

I nodded. I was gone.

Up into the mountains now. Far. Far. The sky was a bucket of ice in which no moons floated. The going became steeper, and the little donkey protested. I whipped him with the throttle and went on. Up. Up. I spotted a green, unwinking star, and felt a lump in my throat. The encased rose beat against my chest like an extra heart. The donkey brayed, long and loudly, then began to cough. I lashed him some more and he died.

I threw the emergency brake on and got out. I began to walk.

So cold, so cold it grows. Up here. At night? Why?

Why did she do it? Why flee the campfire when night comes on?

And I was up, down, around, and through every chasm, gorge, and pass, with my long-legged strides and an ease of movement never known on Earth.

Barely two days remain, my love, and thou hast forsaken me. Why?

I crawled under overhangs. I leaped over ridges. I scraped my knees, an elbow. I heard my jacket tear.

No answer, Malann? Do you really hate your people this much? Then I'll try someone else. Vishnu, you're the Preserver. Preserve her, please! Let me find her.

Jehovah?

Adonis? Osiris? Thammuz? Manitou? Legba? Where is she?

I ranged far and high, and I slipped.

Stones ground underfoot and I dangled over an edge. My fingers so cold. It was hard to grip the rock.

I looked down.

Twelve feet or so. I let go and dropped, landed rolling.

Then I heard her scream.

I lay there, not moving, looking up. Against the night, above, she called.

"Gallinger!"

I lay still.

"Gallinger!"

And she was gone.

I heard stones rattle and knew she was coming down some path to the right of me.

I jumped up and ducked into the shadow of a boulder.

She rounded a cutoff, and picked her way, uncertainly, through the stones.

"Gallinger?"

I stepped out and seized her shoulders.

"Braxa."

She screamed again, then began to cry, crowding against me. It was the first time I had ever heard her cry.

"Why?" I asked. "Why?"

But she only clung to me and sobbed.

Finally, "I thought you had killed yourself."

"Maybe I would have," I said. "Why did you leave Tirellian? And me?"

"Didn't M'Cwyie tell you? Didn't you guess?"

"I didn't guess, and M'Cwyie said she didn't know."

"Then she lied. She knows."

"What? What is it she knows?"

She shook all over, then was silent for a long time. I realized suddenly that she was wearing only her flimsy dancer's costume. I pushed her from me, took off my jacket, and put it about her shoulders.

"Great Malann!" I cried. "You'll freeze to death!"

"No," she said, "I won't."

I was transferring the rose-case to my pocket.

"What is that?" she asked.

"A rose," I answered. "You can't make it out much in the dark. I once compared you to one. Remember?"

"Ye-Yes. May I carry it?"

"Sure." I stuck it in the jacket pocket.

"Well? I'm still waiting for an explanation."

"You really do not know?" she asked.

"No!"

"When the Rains came," she said, "apparently only our men were affected, which was enough. . . . Because I—wasn't—affected—apparently—"

"Oh," I said. "Oh."

We stood there, and I thought.

"Well, why did you run? What's wrong with being pregnant on Mars? Tamur was mistaken. Your people can live again."

She laughed, again that wild violin played by a

Paginini gone mad. I stopped her before it went too far.

"How?" she finally asked, rubbing her cheek.

"Your people live longer than ours. If our child is normal it will mean our races can intermarry. There must still be other fertile women of your race. Why not?"

"You have read the Book of Locar," she said, "and yet you ask me that? Death was decided, voted upon, and passed, shortly after it appeared in this form. But long before, the followers of Locar knew. They decided it long ago. 'We have done all things,' they said, 'we have seen all things, we have heard and felt all things. The dance was good. Now let it end.' "

"You can't believe that."

"What I believe does not matter," she replied. "M'Cwyie and the Mothers have decided we must die. Their very title is now a mockery, but their decisions will be upheld. There is only one prophecy left, and it is mistaken. We will die."

"No," I said.

"What, then?"

"Come back with me, to Earth."

"No."

"All right, then. Come with me now."

"Where?"

"Back to Tirellian. I'm going to talk to the Mothers."

"You can't! There is a Ceremony tonight!"

I laughed.

"A ceremony for a god who knocks you down, and then kicks you in the teeth?"

"He is still Malann," she answered. "We are still his people."

"You and my father would have gotten along fine," I snarled. "But I am going, and you are coming with me, even if I have to carry you—and I'm bigger than you are."

"But you are not bigger than Ontro."

"Who the hell is Ontro?"

"He will stop you, Gallinger. He is the Fist of Malann."

IV

I scudded the jeepster to a halt in front of the only entrance I knew, M'Cwyie's. Braxa, who had seen the rose in a headlamp, now cradled it in her lap, like our child, and said nothing. There was a passive, lovely look on her face.

"Are they in the Temple now?" I wanted to know.

The Madonna-expression did not change. I repeated the question. She stirred.

"Yes," she said, from a distance, "but you cannot go in."

"We'll see."

I circled and helped her down.

I led her by the hand, and she moved as if in a trance. In the light of the new-risen moon, her eyes looked as they had the day I met her, when she had danced. I snapped my fingers. Nothing happened.

So I pushed the door open and led her in. The room was half-lighted.

And she screamed for the third time that evening:

"Do not harm him, Ontro! It is Gallinger!"

I had never seen a Martian man before, only women. So I had no way of knowing whether he was a freak, though I suspected it strongly.

I looked up at him.

His half-naked body was covered with moles and swellings. Gland trouble, I guessed.

I had thought I was the tallest man on the planet, but he was seven feet tall and overweight. Now I knew where my giant bed had come from!

"Go back," he said. "She may enter. You may not."

"I must get my books and things."

He raised a huge left arm. I followed it. All my belongings lay neatly stacked in the corner.

"I must go in. I must talk with M'Cwyie and the Mothers."

"You may not."

"The lives of your people depend on it."

"Go back," he boomed. "Go home to *your* people, Gallinger. Leave *us!*"

My name sounded so different on his lips, like someone else's. How old was he? I wondered. Three hundred? Four? Had he been a Temple guardian all his life? Why? Who was there to guard against? I didn't like the way he moved. I had seen men who moved like that before.

"Go back," he repeated.

If they had refined their martial arts as far as they had their dances, or, worse yet, if their fighting arts were a part of the dance, I was in for trouble.

"Go on in," I said to Braxa. "Give the rose to M'Cwyie. Tell her that I sent it. Tell her I'll be there shortly."

"I will do as you ask. Remember me on Earth, Gallinger. Good-bye."

I did not answer her, and she walked past Ontro and into the next room, bearing her rose.

"Now will you leave?" he asked. "If you like, I will tell her that we fought and you almost beat me, but I knocked you unconscious and carried you back to your ship."

"No," I said, "either I go around you or go over you, but I am going through."

He dropped into a crouch, arms extended.

"It is a sin to lay hands on a holy man," he rumbled, "but I will stop you, Gallinger."

My memory was a fogged window, suddenly exposed to fresh air. Things cleared. I looked back six years.

I was a student of Oriental Languages at the University of Tokyo. It was my twice-weekly night of recreation. I stood in a thirty-foot circle in the Kodokan, the *judogi* lashed about my high hips by a brown belt. I was *Ik-kyu*, one notch below the lowest degree of expert. A brown diamond above my right breast said "Jiu-Jitsu" in Japanese, and it meant *atemiwaza*, really, because of the one striking-technique I had worked out, found unbelievably suitable to my size, and won matches with.

But I had never used it on a man, and it was five years since I had practiced. I was out of shape, I knew, but I tried hard to force my mind *tsuki no kokoro*, like the moon, reflecting the all of Ontro.

Somewhere, out of the past, a voice said, "*Hajime*, let it begin."

I snapped into my *neko-ashi-dachi* cat-stance, and his eyes burned strangely. He hurried to correct his own position—and I threw it at him!

My one trick!

My long left leg lashed up like a broken spring. Seven feet off the ground my foot connected with his jaw as he tried to leap backward.

His head snapped back and he fell. A soft moan escaped his lips. *That's all there is to it*, I thought. *Sorry, old fellow.*

And as I stepped over him, somehow, groggily, he tripped me, and I fell across his body. I couldn't believe he had strength enough to remain conscious after that blow, let alone move. I hated to punish him any more.

But he found my throat and slipped a forearm across it before I realized there was a purpose to his action.

No! Don't let it end like this!

It was a bar of steel across my windpipe, my carotids. Then I realized that he was still unconscious, and that this was a reflex instilled by countless years of training. I had seen it happen once, in *shiai*. The man died because he had been choked unconscious and still fought on, and his opponent thought he had not been applying the choke properly. He tried harder.

But it was rare, so very rare!

I jammed my elbows into his ribs and threw my head back in his face. The grip eased, but not enough. I hated to do it, but I reached up and broke his little finger.

The arm went loose and I twisted free.

He lay there panting, face contorted. My heart went out to the fallen giant, defending his people, his religion, following his orders. I cursed myself as I had never cursed before, for walking over him, instead of around.

I staggered across the room to my little heap of possessions. I sat on the projector case and lit a cigarette.

I couldn't go into the Temple until I got my breath back, until I thought of something to say.

How do you talk a race out of killing itself?

Suddenly—

—Could it happen? Would it work that way? If I read them the Book of Ecclesiastes—if I read them a greater piece of literature than any Locar ever wrote—and as somber—and as pessimistic—and showed them that our race had gone on despite one man's condemning all of life in the highest poetry—showed them that the vanity he had mocked had borne us to the Heavens—would they believe it—would they change their minds?

I ground out my cigarette on the beautiful floor, and found my notebook. A strange fury rose within me as I stood.

And I walked into the Temple to preach the Black Gospel according to Gallinger, from the Book of Life.

* * *

There was silence all about me.

M'Cwyie had been reading Locar, the rose set at her right hand, target of all eyes.

Until I entered.

Hundreds of people were seated on the floor, barefoot. The few men were as small as the women, I noted.

I had my boots on.

Go all the way, I figured. *You either lose or you win—everything!*

A dozen crones sat in a semicircle behind M'Cwyie. The Mothers.

The barren earth, the dry wombs, the fire-touched.

I moved to the table.

"Dying yourselves, you would condemn your people," I addressed them, "that they may not know the life you have known—the joys, the sorrows, the fullness—but it is not true that you all must die." I addressed the multitude now. "Those who say this lie. Braxa knows, for she will bear a child—"

They sat there, like rows of Buddhas. M'Cwyie drew back into the semicircle.

"—my child!" I continued, wondering what my father would have thought of this sermon.

". . . And all the women young enough may bear children. It is only your men who are sterile. And if you permit the doctors of the next expedition to examine you, perhaps even the men may be helped. But if they cannot, you can mate with the men of Earth.

"And ours is not an insignificant people, an insignificant place," I went on. "Thousands of years ago, the Locar of our world wrote a book saying that it was. He spoke as Locar did, but we did not lie down, despite plagues, wars, and famines. We did not die. One by one we beat down the diseases, we fed the hungry, we fought the wars, and, recently, have gone a long time without them. We may finally have conquered them. I do not know.

"But we have crossed millions of miles of nothingness.

We have visited another world. And our Locar had said, 'Why bother? What is the worth of it? It is all vanity, anyhow.'

"And the secret is," I lowered my voice, as at a poetry reading, "he was right! It *is* vanity; it *is* pride! It is the hubris of rationalism to always attack the prophet, the mystic, the god. It is our blasphemy which has made us great, and will sustain us, and which the gods secretly admire in us. And the truly sacred names of God are blasphemous things to speak!"

I was working up a sweat. I paused dizzily.

"Here is the Book of Ecclesiastes," I announced, and began:

"'Vanity of vanities, saith the Preacher, vanity of vanities; all is vanity. What profit hath a man . . .'"

I spotted Braxa in the back, mute, rapt.

I wondered what she was thinking.

And I wound the hours of night about me, like black thread on a spool.

Oh it was late! I had spoken till day came, and still I spoke. I finished Ecclesiastes and continued Gallinger.

And when I finished there was still only a silence.

The Buddhas, all in a row, had not stirred through the night. And after a long while M'Cwyie raised her right hand. One by one the Mothers did the same.

And I knew what that meant.

It meant no, do not, cease, and stop.

It meant that I had failed.

I walked slowly from the room and slumped beside my baggage.

Ontro was gone. Good that I had not killed him. . . .

After a thousand years M'Cwyie entered.

She said, "Your job is finished."

I did not move.

"The prophecy is fulfilled," she said. "My people are rejoicing. You have won, holy man. Now leave us quickly."

My mind was a deflated balloon. I pumped a little air back into it.

"I'm not a holy man," I said, "just a second-rate poet with a bad case of hubris."

I lit my last cigarette.

Finally, "All right, what prophecy?"

"The Promise of Locar," she replied, as though the explaining were unnecessary, "that a holy man would come from the Heavens to save us in our last hours, if all the dances of Locar were completed. He would defeat the Fist of Malann and bring us life."

"How?"

"As with Braxa, and as the example in the Temple."

"Example?"

"You read us his words, as great as Locar's. You read to us how there is 'nothing new under the sun.' And you mocked his words as you read them—showing us a new thing.

"There has never been a flower on Mars," she said, "but we will learn to grow them.

"You are the Sacred Scoffer," she finished. "He-Who-Must-Mock-in-the-Temple—you go shod on holy ground."

"But you voted 'no,' " I said.

"I voted not to carry out our original plan, and to let Braxa's child live instead."

"Oh." The cigarette fell from my fingers. How close it had been! How little I had known!

"And Braxa?"

"She was chosen half a Process ago to do the dances—to wait for you."

"But she said that Ontro would stop me."

M'Cwyie stood there for a long time.

"She had never believed the prophecy herself. Things are not well with her now. She ran away, fearing it was true. When you completed it and we voted, she knew."

"Then she does not love me? Never did?"

"I am sorry, Gallinger. It was the one part of her duty she never managed."

"Duty," I said flatly. . . . Dutydutyduty! Tra-la!

"She has said good-bye; she does not wish to see you again.

". . . and we will never forget your teachings," she added.

"Don't," I said, automatically, suddenly knowing the great paradox which lies at the heart of all miracles. I did not believe a world of my own gospel, never had.

I stood, like a drunken man, and muttered "M'narra."

I went outside, into my last day on Mars.

I have conquered thee, Malann—and the victory is thine! Rest easy on thy starry bed. God damned!

I left the jeepster there and walked back to the *Aspic,* leaving the burden of life so many footsteps behind me. I went to my cabin, locked the door, and took forty-four sleeping pills.

But when I awakened I was in the dispensary, and alive.

I felt the throb of engines as I slowly stood up and somehow made it to the port.

Blurred Mars hung like a swollen belly above me, until it dissolved, brimmed over, and steamed down my face.

JOHN DALMAS
He's done it all!

John Dalmas has just about done it all—parachute infantryman, army medic, stevedore, merchant seaman, logger, smokejumper, administrative forester, farm worker, creamery worker, technical writer, free-lance editor—and his experience is reflected in his writing. His marvelous sense of nature and wilderness combined with his high-tech world view involves the reader with his very real characters. For lovers of fast-paced action-adventures!

THE REGIMENT
The planet Tyss is so poor that it has only one resource: its fighting men. Each year three regiments are sent forth into the galaxy. And once a regiment is constituted, it never recruits again: as casualties mount the regiment becomes a battalion . . . a company . . . a platoon . . . a squad . . . and then there are none. But after the last man of *this* regiment has flung himself into battle, the Federation of Worlds will never be the same!

THE WHITE REGIMENT
All the Confederation of Worlds wanted was a little peace. So they applied their personnel selection technology to war and picked the greatest potential warriors out of their planets-wide database of psych profiles. And they hired the finest mercenaries in the galaxy to train the first test regiment—they hired the legendary black warriors of Tyss to create the first ever White Regiment.

THE KALIF'S WAR
The White Regiment had driven back the soldiers of the Kharganik empire, but the Kalif was certain that

he could succeed in bringing the true faith of the Prophet of Kargh to the Confederation—even if he had to bombard the infidels' planets with nuclear weapons to do it! But first he would have to thwart a conspiracy in his own ranks that was planning to replace him with a more tractable figurehead...

FANGLITH
Fanglith was a near-mythical world to which criminals and misfits had been exiled long ago. The planet becomes all too real to Larn and Deneen when they track their parents there, and find themselves in the middle of the Age of Chivalry on a world that will one day be known as Earth.

RETURN TO FANGLITH
The oppressive Empire of Human Worlds, temporarily filed in *Fanglith*, has struck back and resubjugated its colony planets. Larn and Deneen must again flee their home. Their final object is to reach a rebel base—but the first stop is Fanglith!

THE LIZARD WAR
A thousand years after World War III and Earth lies supine beneath the heel of a gang of alien sociopaths who like to torture whole populations for sport. But while the 16th century level of technology the aliens found was relatively easy to squelch, the mystic warrior sects that had evolved in the meantime weren't....

THE LANTERN OF GOD
They were pleasure droids, designed for maximum esthetic sensibility and appeal, abandoned on a deserted planet after catastrophic systems failure on their transport ship. After 2000 years undisturbed, "real" humans arrive on the scene—and 2000 thousand years of droid freedom is about to come to a sharp and bloody end.

THE REALITY MATRIX
Is the existence we call life on Earth for real, or is it a game? Might Earth be an artificial construct designed by a group of higher beings? Is everything an illusion? Everything is—except the Reality Matrix. And what if self-appointed "Lords of Chaos" place a chaos generator in the matrix, just to see what will happen? Answer: The slow destruction of our world.

THE GENERAL'S PRESIDENT
The stock market crash of 1994 makes Black Monday of 1929 look like a minor market adjustment—and the fabric of society is torn beyond repair. The Vice President resigns under a cloud of scandal—and when the military hints that they may let the lynch mobs through anyway, the President resigns as well. So the Generals get to pick a President. But the man they choose turns out to be more of a leader than they bargained for....

Available at your local bookstore. Or you can order any or all of John Dalmas' books with this order form. Just check your choice(s) below and send the combined cover price to: Baen Books, Dept. BA, P.O. Box 1403, Riverdale, NY 10471.

THE REGIMENT • 416 pp. • 72065-1 • $4.95 _____

THE WHITE REGIMENT • 416 pp. • 69880-X • $3.95 _____

THE KALIF'S WAR • 416 pp. • 72062-7 • $4.95 _____

FANGLITH • 256 pp. • 55988-5 • $2.95 _____

RETURN TO FANGLITH • 288 pp. • 65343-1 • $2.95 _____

THE LIZARD WAR • 320 pp. • 69851-6 • $3.95 _____

THE LANTERN OF GOD • 416 pp. • 69821-4 • $3.95 _____

THE REALITY MATRIX • 352 pp. • 65583-3 • $2.95 _____

THE GENERAL'S PRESIDENT • 384 pp. • 65384-9 • $3.50 _____

Anne McCaffrey
vs.
The Planet Pirates

SASSINAK: Sassinak was twelve when the raiders came. That made her just the right age: old enough to be used, young enough to be broken. But Sassinak turned out to be a little different from your typical slave girl. And finally, she escaped. But that was only the beginning for Sassinak. Now she's a fleet captain with a pirate-chasing ship of her own, and only one regret in life: not enough pirates.
BY ANNE MCCAFFREY AND ELIZABETH MOON
69863 * $4.95 _____

THE DEATH OF SLEEP: Lunzie Mespil was a Healer. All she wanted in life was a chance to make things better for others. But she was getting the feeling she was particularly marked by fate: every ship she served on ran into trouble—and every time she went out, she ended up in coldsleep. When she went to the Dinosaur Planet she thought the curse was lifted—but there she met a long-lost relative named *Sassinak* who'd make her life much more complicated. . . .
BY ANNE MCCAFFREY AND JODY LYNN NYE
69884-2 * $4.95 _____

GENERATION WARRIORS: Sassinak and Lunzie combine forces to beat the planet pirates once and for all. With Lunzie's contacts, Sassinak's crew, and Sassinak herself, it would take a galaxy-wide conspiracy to foil them. Unfortunately, that's just what the planet pirates are. . . .
BY ANNE MCCAFFREY AND ELIZABETH MOON
72041-4 * $4.95 _____

Available at your local bookstore. Or you can order any or all of these books with this order form. Just mark your choices above and send the combined cover price/s to: Baen Books, Dept. BA, P.O. Box 1403, Riverdale, NY 10471.

ANNE McCAFFREY
ELIZABETH MOON

Sassinak was twelve when the raiders came. That made her just the right age: old enough to be used, young enough to be broken. Or so the slavers thought. But Sassy turned out to be a little different from your typical slave girl. Maybe it was her unusual physical strength. Maybe it was her friendship with the captured Fleet crewman. Maybe it was her spirit. Whatever it was, it wouldn't let her resign herself to the life of a slave. She bided her time, watched for her moment. Finally it came, and she escaped. But that was only the beginning for Sassinak. Now she's a Fleet captain with a pirate-chasing ship of her own, and only one regret in her life: not enough pirates.

SASSINAK

You're going to love her!

Coming in March, from
BAEN BOOKS

A ROSE FOR ECCLESIASTES

Up into the mountains now. Far. Far. The sky was a bucket of ice in which no moons floated. The going became steeper, and the little donkey protested. I whipped him with the throttle and went on. Up. Up. I spotted a green, unwinking star, and felt a lump in my throat. The encased rose beat against my chest like an extra heart. The donkey brayed, long and loudly, then began to cough. I lashed him some more and he died.

I threw the emergency brake on and got out. I began to walk.

So cold, so cold it grows. Up here. At night? Why? Why did she do it? Why flee the campfire when night comes on?

And I was up, down, around, and through every chasm, gorge, and pass, with my long-legged strides and an ease of movement never known on Earth.

Barely two days remain, my love, and thou hast forsaken me. Why?

I crawled under overhangs. I leaped over ridges. I scraped my knees, an elbow. I heard my jacket tear.

No answer, Malann? Do you really hate your people this much? Then I'll try someone else. Vishnu, you're the Preserver. Preserve her, please! Let me find her.

Jehovah?

Adonis? Osiris? Thammuz? Manitou? Legba? Where is she?

I ranged far and high, and I slipped.

Stones ground underfoot and I dangled over an edge. My fingers so cold. It was hard to grip the rock.

I looked down.

Twelve feet or so. I let go and dropped, landed rolling.

Then I heard her scream.